# A WORD FROM THE PUBLISHER

For readers who loved Beth Macy's *Dopesick* and John Berendt's *Midnight in the Garden of Good and Evil*, T*he Dark Water Gospel* delivers a century of Knoxville's hidden history—murders, madams, lynchings, and political machines—narrated through the voice of a woman who knew where all the bones were buried.

# THE DARK WATER
# GOSPEL

SCAN THE QR CODE BELOW TO JOIN THE PREMIUM PULP FICTION SUBSTACK. YOU'LL GET ACCESS TO EARLY CHAPTERS, PODCAST EPISODES, NEW RELEASES, AND MEMBER PERKS.

YOU'LL ALSO GET EARLY ACCESS TO EVERY NEW PREMIUM PULP FICTION TITLE.

NO SPAM. UNSUBSCRIBE ANYTIME.

IF THE CODE WON'T SCAN, PLEASE VISIT:
WWW.CITIZENONE.WORLD/PREMIUMPULP

# THE DARK WATER
# GOSPEL

## AN EAST TENNESSEE ANTHOLOGY

### BY
### DOUGLAS STUART MCDANIEL

**Premium Pulp Fiction Books**
www.citizenone.world

SAVANNAH | OCEAN SPRINGS | BARCELONA

Copyright © 2026 Douglas Stuart McDaniel  All rights reserved.

Thank you for purchasing an authorized edition of this book and for complying with copyright law. No part of this book may be reproduced, stored in a retrieval system, or transmitted by any means, electronic, mechanical, photocopying, recording, or otherwise, without written permission from the copyright holder.

This work is being published and distributed under the Premium Pulp Fiction imprint.

For ordering information or special discounts for bulk purchases, please contact Premium Pulp Fiction at: 1305 Barnard St #805 Savannah, GA 31401-6746.

Cover design and interior composition by Premium Pulp Fiction
with creative direction by the author.

Publisher's Cataloging-in-Publication data is available.

Print ISBN: 979-8-9935850-3-1

eBook ISBN: 979-8-9935850-6-2

Printed in the United States of America on acid-free paper

25 26 27 28 29 30 31 32    10 9 8 7 6 5 4 3 2 1

First Edition

# DEDICATION

This book is dedicated to my many friends who remain back in Knoxville, Savannah, and Ocean Springs, each city a lens in my forthcoming Southern noir book series.

The real ones, the durable ones, the people who learned early that humor, even dark humor, has always been one of my ways of staying present. Of checking the exits without leaving the room. This is for those who never needed translation, who heard care even when it arrived sideways or laughing at exactly the wrong moment, and who understood that loving a place does not require protecting ourselves from uncomfortable truths.

Some of you stood with me. Some of you stood back. Some of you drifted away when life grew complicated. So did I, I guess. Moved more than 7,000 miles away, first to London, then to the desert of Saudi Arabia for four years, but that's another story.

This book is in memory of Becky French Brewer—my partner in archives, late-night conversations, and long walks through neighborhoods that still remembered what they had been built to hold. She is also the protagonist of this anthology of essays. She offers a masterclass in Appalachian storytelling now, from beyond the grave. Becky understood that history is rarely tidy, that records often fail where memory doesn't, and that refusing to sand down rough edges is sometimes the most honest form of care. She is present in every footnote I didn't write, every joke I didn't explain, and every sequence that mattered more than the moral. If she's reading over my shoulder, she's already telling me to keep going.

This book comes from affection, irritation, memory, and the kind of loyalty that survives clarity. It is for those who recognize themselves in that mix— and for readers who understand why some stories must be told exactly as they are, without smoothing.

With Appalachian affection,
Douglas Stuart McDaniel

*Barcelona, Spain*
March 2026

*Each story in this anthology draws on recollections shaped by memory. Some identifying details may be altered, and dialogue and certain events are unapologetically recreated.*

*This is neither a newsroom nor a courtroom. This is a noir city.*

*The Dark Water Gospel is not concerned with establishing a record of individual acts or adjudicating disputed events. It examines how power operates—how it is exercised, protected, and remembered—within a particular time and place.*

# CONTENTS

DEDICATION ................................................................... vii
PROLOGUE ......................................................................... 1

ONE: THE MCGHEE-CAPONE AFFAIR .............................. 3
TWO: POETRY SLAM ...................................................... 13
THREE: LAST CHRISTMAS IN HOLSTON HILLS ............. 23
FOUR: THE JONES-MCGHEE-HOWARD FEUD ................ 31
FIVE: DEAD MAN ON DEPOT ......................................... 53
SIX: THE MADAM AND THE TRASH CAN ....................... 59
SEVEN: LYNCH MOB ON THE GAY STREET BRIDGE ..... 67
EIGHT: WHAT THIS TOWN COULD TOLERATE .............. 73
NINE: KINGPIN ............................................................... 79
TEN: THE RIVER SECRETS OF PETER BLOW ................. 93
ELEVEN: BLUEBLOODS ON THE BUS ........................... 103
TWELVE: STILL TRYIN' TO SIGN OFF ........................... 113
THIRTEEN: RED SUMMER ............................................ 119
FOURTEEN: OPERATION AQUARIUS ........................... 127
FIFTEEN: THIS IS NOT A TOUPÉE ................................ 137

ABOUT THE AUTHOR ................................................... 153

> "There is nothing beautiful about the wreckage of a human being. There is nothing pretty about damage, about pain, about heartache. What is beautiful is their strength, their resilience, their fortitude as they display an ocean of courage when they pick through the wreckage of their life to build something beautiful brand new, against every odd that is stacked against them."
>
> — Nikita Gill, *Wreckage*

# PROLOGUE

Knoxville learned early how to manage its reputation. Not through headlines, which were always edited carefully, but through quieter channels: courthouse hallways where a familiar name altered the room, lodge basements where charity and gambling nights shared the same calendar, porches where stories waited until discretion loosened and laughter took over. Decisions were made without minutes. Accountability, when it arrived, arrived late. What survived was called tradition, and sometimes history.

Names do real work across the Tennessee Valley. They opened doors and closed investigations. They crossed town lines and returned with added weight. Some names circulated as credentials; others functioned as warnings. Readers will encounter both. The mechanics are consistent: who is related to whom, who once helped whom, who is owed, who can be trusted to stay quiet. These details rarely appeared in print, but they governed outcomes all the same.

This book assembles a record from what was preserved, remembered, and omitted, drawing on court files, police reports, planning documents, news clippings, and oral accounts never archived. Its focus is not spectacle, but process: how decisions were routed, responsibility deferred, and public language used to soften private actions.

The stories that follow track a consistent pattern. A signature appears where it should not. A feud migrates from a legal dispute to a public shooting. A sheriff enforces the law selectively and is eventually forced to enforce it on familiar faces. Respectability absorbs damage and continues to function. When consequences arrive, they are framed as anomalies rather than outcomes.

Some figures recur as operators—people fluent in discretion, who understood which conversations mattered and which did not.

Others appear as reformers, often briefly, and often at cost. There are storytellers tasked with smoothing edges, redirecting attention, or translating misconduct into civic pride. There are neighborhoods repeatedly asked to wait their turn. These roles are not unique to Knoxville, but the local arrangements give them particular form.

This is not a nostalgic book, and it is not an exposé. It does not argue that the city is uniquely corrupt, nor does it claim comprehensive coverage. It examines how civic memory is managed, how misconduct adapts its presentation, and how loyalty can outlast evidence. Knoxville is the setting, not the exception. The mechanisms on display will be familiar to anyone who has watched a Southern city protect its image while quietly rearranging the facts.

No one is redeemed in these pages. The interest here is not moral closure but documentation. When wrongdoing is acknowledged, it is often contained. When harm is addressed, it is frequently reclassified. Patterns are treated as isolated incidents. Language does the hard work.

Readers are asked to proceed as they would through a file. Pay attention to where names recur and where they disappear. Note which addresses are described and which are skipped. When a project is announced as renewal, look for who was displaced. When an incident is labeled unfortunate, look for how often similar incidents have been labeled the same way before.

Each story can be traced back to verifiable sources for those inclined to check. The accounts are shaped for clarity rather than absolution. The aim is not to straighten events into a single narrative, but to present them accurately enough that their alignment becomes visible.

If there is a shared plot, it is procedural. Respectability functions as a local language of permission. Geography operates as character. Streets, neighborhoods, and institutions appear repeatedly, performing the same roles under different circumstances. Outcomes change less than explanations do.

The book begins with a borrowed name, a forged signature, and a Knoxville family unexpectedly connected to a New York gangland murder. The details are ordinary. The routing is not.

## One

# THE MCGHEE-CAPONE AFFAIR

Becky French Brewer had a lead on a big story, and sitting on my front porch in Old North Knoxville late one evening, she pitched it to me. It was long after the lightning bugs had clocked out and I was staring at the bottom of an empty bottle of bourbon.

I can't remember the year exactly: we were celebrating a local election win, and the evening was going late, but she was already changing the subject. She didn't have all the facts yet, but trusted me to help her with the research.

Swapping old Knoxville crime and murder stories until midnight and beyond had become habit—local scandals, murder ballads, and every half-true rumor from Sharp's Ridge to the river. Becky had a memory that polished everything it touched.

We wrote together sometimes—a book about Park City, some stage plays, and stories that lived somewhere between the archives and the afterlife. When she passed in 2017, my front porch went quiet. Knoxville lost one of its best keepers of mischief and memory.

Becky would have loved how I finally stitched this tale together—the flannel cutter, the borrowed name, the Nash that went north and came back in headlines. She'd have known where all the bones were buried and who buried them. So, Becky, wherever you're swapping stories tonight—maybe with the ghosts of the McGhees or Frankie Yale himself—this one's for you.

I still miss your laughter, your stubbornness, your corrections, and the way you could turn a bad idea into a good story—before the coffee got cold.

Here's to the storytellers—those who stayed, those who strayed, and those who keep the porch lights on for the rest of us.

· · ·

**January, 1928.** The Farragut Hotel stood at the corner of Gay Street and Clinch Avenue, its marble columns polished by less than two decades of wealthy elbows. Inside, tobacco and bergamot cologne tangled with the faint scent of fried oysters drifting up from the café below. The brass elevator clanged open and shut, each arrival ushering in men with soft hands and loud wallets. Upstairs, behind a door etched PRIVATE, the city's commerce ran on whiskey and pretense. The fan hummed overhead.

John M. McGhee wasn't supposed to be there. He'd come at the invitation of a wholesale garment buyer who drank much more than he ordered, a man who skipped introductions. The knitting mill where John worked was closed for inventory, and he had been glad for the excuse to trade the smell of oilcloth and flannel dust for cigar smoke and a hint of danger. He was a flannel cutter by trade—sharp knives, measured patience, a man who traced the same outlines a hundred times a day until the muscle remembered for him.

He'd been told he had "a good hand," which is how men talk you into using it.

The others assumed more. A few whispered questions had traveled the table early on—McGhee, like the library? The new airport under construction out in Blount County? John smiled and said nothing. The truth was duller: a rented house on Atkin Street, a wife who mended for neighbors, a father who tended land out in Trentville. He had no library, no stock portfolio, only a pair of good shoes and a name that carried echoes of marble and railroads. In Knoxville, that was often enough.

The game started harmless—nickel antes, polite laughter, stories about trips to Louisville and bad whiskey in Asheville. The dealer was a lanky man with preacher's hands who shuffled with a reverence that made sin feel orderly. Then the rye started to flow from a silver flask passed under the table, and the stakes grew in quiet increments: nickels to quarters, quarters to dollars, dollars to tens. Each raise sounded small until the pile on the felt could have paid a man's wages for a year.

John held on, half-lucky, half-blind. The fabric buyer had long folded, and the Louisville salesman had started calling him Mr. McGhee in a tone that was both mocking and admiring. The dealer's grin was narrow and unreadable. The radiator ticked, the fan turned slow, and the whiskey made everything shimmer.

When the last hand came, the room had gone reverent. John's cards looked good—a queen-high straight, tidy and hopeful—and for one foolish heartbeat he imagined leaving the cutting table behind. He raised, the salesman matched, and then the dealer laid down his spread with the calm grace of a clerk closing the till. A straight flush—perfect, merciless. The chips slid across the felt like a tide going out, and with them went John's borrowed ease.

He felt the color drain from his face as the others chuckled. Someone poured him another drink, and he took it without tasting. He could still smell the chemical sweetness of the flannel factory on his cuffs, mixed now with cigar smoke and sweat. The Louisville man tapped his cigarette, leaned forward, and said, "Hell of a run, Mr. McGhee. A man with your name will land on his feet."

John laughed once—thin, not quite his own. A promissory note on hotel stationery was pressed into his hand, and he signed. He wrote it in a looping hand, the way he'd practiced his signature as a boy, as if a better version of himself might answer to it. The pen scratched across the paper; the dealer folded the IOU and slid it into his vest pocket.

Outside, Gay Street was all reflection—neon in the puddles, the Sterchi Brothers' warehouse glowing down the block, Woodruff's electric sign promising STYLE FOR THE MODERN FAMILY. He walked past the white marble of the Lawson McGhee Library on Vine and Walnut, where his supposed kin's philanthropy glowed in lamplight.

The name carved in its pediment looked holy and foreign, like something borrowed from someone else's dream. He thought of the Tysons, who'd lost a son in the war and were already talking about building an airfield in his honor. McGhee Tyson Field, they called it—a monument to sacrifice, built on land no working man could afford to lose.

Names had altitude in Knoxville; his just scraped the ground. By the time he reached Atkin Street, the respect that had always felt like a birthright now pressed on him like a weight.

Cora was waiting by the window, hair pinned, mending in her lap. She looked up, saw his face, and didn't ask. When he told her, she set down the needle and said, "We'll manage." He wanted to believe her. But the sound of the cards still rang in his head, the dealer's quiet voice still calling him Mr. McGhee, and he knew something in him had already been sold.

He undressed in silence, laid his coat over the chair, and stood at the window watching the city's veins of light stretch out across the river. The Holston Bank Tower's white stone caught the moonlight, a monument to other McGhees' ambition. He could not sleep. He kept seeing the table, the cards, the neat little IOU—his name on paper, proof that even a good man could be mistaken for the McGhee who could afford to lose.

...

He woke to a knock at the door the next morning—too polite to be the landlord, too confident to be a neighbor. Standing there was a man in a dark coat, hat tipped low, watching John guess. He smelled of Lucky Strikes and bank lobbies.

"Name's Cox," he said, stepping in before he was invited. He put his hat on the table, looked around the room, and let his eyes rest on John the way a surveyor measures a property line.

"You lost at the Farragut," he said. No question mark, no judgment.

Cox wasn't a man who threatened; he didn't have to. He had the calm of somebody who knew how a man's bad decisions could be repurposed.

"I got a way to fix it," he said. "Simple. You order a Nash."

John blinked. "A car? I…I can't afford a car."

Cox smiled. "Use your name. McGhee's a solid name in this town. Dealers hear that, they start adding zeroes to the trust column. You sign the papers, then hand over the keys. My people handle delivery—Atlanta way—you get your debt cleared, your wife stops worrying, and everybody sleeps easier."

He said it like he was describing how to hang wallpaper—no sin in it, just procedure. John listened because the rhythm of that card shuffle still lived behind his eyes, and because Cora had already started saving candle wax to stretch the light.

Cox spoke quietly. "That salesman down there won't ask if you cut flannel or own the factory. All he'll see is a McGhee with good shoes and a pen. A name like yours moves pencils."

John understood: the world was built by men who could make paper lie with implied prestige.

The next day he walked into the Nash dealership with the posture of a man trying on confidence. He gave his name and address—505 Atkin Street—and left the occupation line blank. He'd thought about writing "plant manager," but his mama had taught him not to lie, at least not on paper. The salesman believed it. The name McGhee did the heavy lifting.

They shook hands, and John signed where he was told. The salesman's smile was all teeth and commission. In the back room, a courier who looked allergic to daylight counted a stack of bills and slipped them into a plain envelope. "Debt cleared," he said, and John felt the relief before the shame.

Cox never said the word "illegal". Everything had paperwork: bill of sale, temporary plate, dealer's transit permit, a clean title printed on fresh bond paper. The dirt lived under the ink.

As they finished, Cox picked up his hat, brushed an invisible speck from the brim, and smiled. "We'll leave the Tennessee plate on," he said. "Names travel. Sometimes they're useful when they need to be."

John didn't ask what he meant. He didn't want to. He just wanted that IOU burned, his name quiet again, and his life small enough to fit back inside his own pockets.

• • •

Before men came to collect the car, John and Cora decided to steal something back from fate: one joyride, paid for in bad judgment and borrowed time.

He told her they were "just checking the alignment," which Cora understood to mean he needed to feel like someone else for a few miles. She put on her Sunday hat anyway, because if you're going to sin, you might as well look decent doing it.

They slid into the Nash like they were sneaking into a church pew after the sermon had started. The motor purred, low and civilized, as if it knew how far above their station it sat. The heater coughed on like an old dog, and for once in their marriage, John didn't mind the smell of gasoline—it smelled like permission.

They rolled over the Gay Street Bridge, opened in 1898 when John and Cora were two years old. The old steel spine hummed under the tires. The Tennessee River below caught every light in Knoxville and dragged it west, slow as a sermon. On the far side, South Knoxville waited—dark roads, hound dogs, and moonlight over barns that hadn't been painted since Taft.

John opened it up to forty, maybe fifty, wind cutting through the half-open window and whipping Cora's hat ribbon like it was trying to escape. She laughed once—sharp, surprised, forgiving. "You trying to kill us or impress me?" she shouted over the wind.

"Little of both!" he hollered back, grinning like a man with money in his pocket and no sense in his head.

They took the old Sevierville Pike until the lamps gave up, then coasted down a gravel ridge where the whole town glowed faintly behind them—factories, church steeples, and the bright lie of civilization. He killed the engine, and for a moment it was just the tick of the cooling motor and the sound of a whippoorwill judging them from the trees.

Cora leaned against him, her hand on his arm. "Feels like we ought to thank somebody for this."

"Go ahead," he said. "But maybe don't use my name."

She laughed again, softer, and rested her head against his shoulder. The Nash, sleek and borrowed, sat under the stars. For one night, John wasn't a flannel cutter with a crooked ledger; he was a man who had done right by his wife, which is about as close as most men get to redemption.

They rolled home before dawn, the headlights tracing the porches of Atkin Street. Curtains twitched. A few neighbors nodded, deciding maybe the McGhees weren't that kind of poor after all.

John parked the Nash out front, the hood gleaming like new money. He sat for a second, watching the sunrise catch the chrome, and thought maybe Cox's cash wasn't all bad—it had bought him one good night, a wife's laughter, and the brief illusion of having climbed his own name. He left the key in the ignition, walked Cora inside, and didn't look back.

In Knoxville, that night was more than most men stole. At daybreak, John watched a man walk up and drive his dream away.

He swore off poker.

• • •

**July 1, 1928 — Brooklyn, New York.** Five months later, the Nash rolled back into the world like bad karma on four tires. It was a Sunday, hot enough to make even crooks sweat. At three in the afternoon, a black sedan eased up behind a Lincoln on Forty-Fourth Street in Brooklyn's Bath Beach. Inside the Lincoln sat Francesco "Frankie" Yale, florist by trade, gangster by calling, the man who had once taught a younger Al Capone how to collect money without getting his cuffs dirty.

The sedan pulled alongside, windows down, nothing said. Then the first Thompson opened up—short, percussive. Witnesses swore they counted nearly a hundred rounds. Yale was driving alone when he was ambushed.

He was hit multiple times by .45-caliber rounds and shotgun fire.

Yale's Lincoln jumped the curb, crashed into the steps of a house at Forty-Fourth Street and New Utrecht Avenue, and sat hissing. When the smoke cleared, Brooklyn had its first machine-gun murder. Capone had mailed his bad manners east.

Police found the black Nash sedan abandoned a few blocks away. Doors flung open, seats shredded, cordite thick in the air. One bullet hole through the steering wheel, three through the windshield, a trail of shell casings in the gutter. And there, plain as day on the back bumper, the Tennessee license plate—the same one that had once rattled across the Gay Street Bridge under John McGhee's hands.

Detectives traced the serial numbers on the Thompsons to a Chicago dealer named Peter von Frantzius—the same man who armed half of Capone's payroll. Another gun led to Parker Henderson Jr. down in Miami, who told a grand jury he'd sold it for "security work." Every clue pointed west toward Chicago.

But what interested the NY Times was the car. RACKETEER YALE SLAIN; MURDER CAR TRACED TO TENNESSEE. They printed the detail as neatly as gospel: "The car was purchased from the Nash agency in Knoxville by a man named Charles Cox and another whose name was not given. They paid $1,050 cash and immediately departed. The car was originally purchased by John McGhee of Atkin Street, Knoxville. The license tag the murder car carried was the one issued to McGhee."

That was the whole chain—three transactions and six degrees of damnation. To the papers it was colorful geography: Chicago, Brooklyn, Knoxville. To John, reading it over breakfast in the dim kitchen on Atkin Street, it was the sound of the universe clearing its throat.

He read the article twice. His hands trembled so badly the coffee slopped onto the table. Cora took the page, folded it along the crease, and smoothed it flat with her palms, the way she did with laundry.

"It can't be ours," she said. But the plate number matched. The title matched. Everything matched except the life they had meant to live.

Cora folded the paper again and slipped it under the flour bin, where the neighbor women wouldn't see it. "Wear your Sunday collar," she said. "Keep your chin up."

Word traveled fast around Knoxville. Neighbors lowered their voices when he passed. The foreman at the mill stopped calling him "Johnny" and went back to "McGhee." The city's better families read the article over breakfast, one eyebrow raised. The name they saw on the page was one they thought they owned, and now it had been caught consorting with Chicago's devils.

John walked to work that Monday under a sky the color of old tin. Every sound—the trolley bell, the hiss of the river below the bridge—mocked him. He'd only tried to settle a debt. Instead he'd leased his name to a murder.

He thought of Cox's parting words: "Names travel."

His had gone all the way to Brooklyn to prove it.

• • •

In the months that followed, John half expected a knock from Knox County Sheriff Chester R. Hackney, the New York police, or a telegram asking him to explain why his name had been connected to a machine-gun murder. For weeks he rehearsed what he might say: that he'd signed a loan agreement, not a conspiracy; that his only crime was believing a man could afford decency on credit.

He kept waiting for the handcuffs, or worse, the story in the Sentinel that would name him "John McGhee, of Atkin Street, connected to the Capone affair."

But nobody came. Not long after, he was out at the mill—fired or forced out, it hardly mattered.

He picked up odd jobs. He sold off the small, invisible things that make a man feel permanent—his sleep, his confidence, his notion that one day he might rise. Cox disappeared, as such men do. Now and then—a flash of a hat brim, a polished shoe stepping into the Holston Bank—but maybe just Knoxville dressing up its ghosts.

The Nash stayed behind like a haunting: a headline here, a paragraph in Pasley's book there, a photograph you could hold to the light and still see the shine on its fenders. His father wrote from Trentville telling him to come home, but John couldn't face the geography of his own mistake. Shame is heavier than luggage, and he'd already packed enough.

Cora died in 1953, quiet as she'd lived. John followed five years later, both laid to rest under a modest stone in Woodlawn Cemetery that read simply MCGHEE. The library downtown kept its grander version of the name carved in marble; the airport over the river carried it on every ticket stub.

The Black McGhees—descendants of the powerful family's forgotten history—carried it with a steadier pride, one earned, not inherited. Sometimes, passing a factory gate, John would nod at one of them and feel, without bitterness, that the name had found better hands.

The road from Atkin Street to Forty-Fourth Street was paved with hotel stationery, bad timing, and a Southern optimism—the belief that good manners could launder anything. It bought him one night of stars and Cora's laughter in a borrowed car, and a lifetime of second thoughts.

The city kept on—East Tennessee marble burnished, airport roaring, ledgers balanced, while departure boards flickered at McGhee Tyson Airport, names rising into the blue sky while his remained earthbound.

But for one winter and a reckless summer, a flannel cutter and his wife drove across the river and believed that a name could take them anywhere.

Two

# POETRY SLAM

Some people never need a nameplate or a gavel to weigh in on a public meeting. Becky French Brewer didn't need to be there to swing the votes. She worked like a stagehand, quiet and fast in the dark, love for the city driving the whole machine. If you knew, you knew. If you didn't, you looked up one morning and a corridor that had been rotting for decades suddenly had a plan attached to it.

"I do my best work in the shadows," she'd say.

I proposed we write a book, the way friends threaten to take a road trip together. Becky didn't need aesthetics to fix a neighborhood. She needed friction—something to catch the gears before the machine rolled on as usual.

IMAGES OF AMERICA: Park City became the book we wrote in 2005, one of those thin local Arcadia Publishing histories, but ours had a sharper edge than most. It was a sepia-toned book that gets shelved in the local history aisle and then keeps walking around town, sold over the counter at Barnes Barber Shop in Burlington, or spinning on a carousel at your interstate Cracker Barrel. It wasn't fancy—no coffee-table gloss. Just names and blocks and detail that refuses nostalgia, that makes people uncomfortable because it insists the past is still standing right where you left it.

I thought if we wrote it down, people might stop calling it "that side of town" or "the gun zone," like it was contagious. Becky already knew that storytelling was a tool of civic imagination—documentation, sure, but also an instrument to pry open necessary conversations.

Ten years later, American Institute of Architects(AIA) Knoxville used the book as source material for their centennial architectural planning study. They traced Magnolia like a scar and started talking about "corridors" and "investment" in the same voice people use for prayer requests. Plans appeared. Meetings multiplied. Then money—real money—showed up and brought its usual entourage: consultants, renderings, and people who'd never walked the blocks they were qualified to improve. Ten million dollars later—give or take a city council meeting—the corridor had begun to see new scaffolding, better lighting, bus stops, and sidewalks. People said we were dreaming if we thought this side of town would get reinvestment.

Becky didn't dream. She called people. She sat in rooms with bad fluorescent lighting and made sure the people in the room didn't get away with pretending the east side was invisible.

She called me late one evening. Around one in the morning. She knew I'd be up.

"Douggie," she said. Soft voice. Knife edge.

I knew that tone. It meant she'd already moved pieces on the board. I happened to be one of them.

"What's the favor?" I asked, bracing for an errand that would end in a meeting that would end in three more meetings.

"I need you to read a poem to the Metropolitan Planning Commission," she said.

"Absolutely not," I said. "I'm not doing open mic at MPC."

She let me hear her grin.

"I'm serious," she said. "There's an item on the agenda—more low-income apartments for East Knoxville, near the zoo. We've talked about this. Developers stand to make a killing off HUD money. The neighborhood needs more market-rate housing. The neighborhood's already drowning in projects and the crime that follows that level of concentrated poverty. West, North, South? They keep batting these things away like flies and we take all the hits. We don't need another box stack with a logo. This neighborhood needs a break."

"You think they hear poems?" I asked.

"They hear from citizens," she said. "And you're a citizen. You'll be speaking for the ones who can't be there at 3:30 pm on a weekday."

That part stuck.

"You'll get five minutes," she added. "And then you'll keep going."

"How long is this poem?"

"Longer than five minutes," she said, and dropped her voice lower. "Whatever they do, you keep reading. I just need you to buy me some time."

I could see the room in my head: the dais, the faces, the microphone with its cold little eye, the timer that blinks like a cheap bomb, the Chair with a gavel nobody wants to hear. I've watched a thousand civic performances and most of them die on the bricks of polite procedure. Becky knew how to jam the gears.

"I feel like Arlo Guthrie on the Group W bench," I said.

"Perfect," she said. "Bring your best outlaw choirboy voice."

She did not explain the rest—not the calls she was already making, not the promises she was already bending. With Becky, the instructions were always surgical: do exactly this, exactly now.

"I'll email the poem," she said. "Print two copies."

"Two?"

"One for you," she said. "And one in case the first one has an unfortunate accident."

I laughed, and she laughed with me, and then the laugh drained out of both of us. I thought of Park City, all those houses like tired lungs. I thought of Magnolia, how long it had been left out in the weather.

"All right," I said. "I'll do it."

"Thank you," she said, and hung up before I could take it back.

I opened her email and began reading. The poem had two moods—plain and pissed. It started with the working day: first shift, second shift, graveyard. It said the names of jobs in a tone that made them sound like hymns—cashier, janitor, nurse aide, bus driver, forklift at the warehouse where the lights never turn all the way off. It asked why meetings that decide the fate of neighborhoods happen at three-thirty in the afternoon on weekdays, when people with hourly jobs can't be there without getting fired. It asked why poor kids have to inherit the overflow of other zip codes' clean conscience. It asked why the word "revitalization" should always feel like a door jammed between two kinds of people—one kind holding the handle with a smile, telling you not to let the door hit you in the ass on your way out of their better zip code.

I read it aloud in my kitchen to nobody, just to see where the air caught. It was long. It took as long as it took. The point wasn't the poem anyway. The point was time.

I printed two copies, slid one behind the other inside a manila folder.

Becky called again.

"Remember," she said, "no matter what."

"No matter what," I said. "Can I go to bed now, your honor?"

• • •

Afternoons in the City-County Building taste like recycled air and paper dust. The elevator opens and you can tell which floor has a fight on it by the static in the hallway. Entering the chamber, I sat with the neighborhood. They knew Becky, of course—every neighborhood knew Becky, even if they didn't know they knew her. I didn't see Becky. That meant she was working. In Knoxville, some people don't need a seat in the room to be heard in it.

The agenda marched along: subdivisions with names like gated moods, a site plan for a medical office that looked like every other medical office. The Chair kept time. People mispronounced street names and corrected themselves with a smile to show they belonged.

The low-income housing project we were trying to kill came up. The developer's man used the usual words: federal support, public-private partnership, units, amenities, community space. He walked the Commissioners through the setbacks and the parking ratios like we were on a polite tour of a polite future. He said the words "affordable housing" and tried to keep his mouth from flinching.

The neighborhood liaison stood and spoke in a calm voice that shook only at the edges. She said they weren't opposed to affordable housing. They were opposed to hundreds more units of concentrated poverty within walking distance of three other complexes that already taxed an exhausted ecosystem—schools, patrol cars, parks, patience. She did not say, "We're a dumping ground," but it hung there anyway.

"Can't we spread these projects into the other zip codes? Share the… wealth? Or lack thereof?"

The liaison didn't raise her voice. She didn't need to. She said what everyone already knew and pretended not to say out loud: projects landed on the east side because land was cheap, resistance was procedural, and the people most affected were at work when the meetings happened. Other neighborhoods had lawyers and design review. This one had sirens, counselors, and patience that kept being tested.

The ask was simple. Build the units—then spread them like you mean it. Share the burden in the zip codes that never have to. Outside the building, the city warned people what crime meant. Inside, it was busy deciding where it would live.

Public comment opened. The timer on the wall glared red numbers. I waited my turn to speak, rose with my folder, walked to the lectern, and placed the first copy of the poem on the flat wood like a small flag.

"Sir," the Chair said. "Name and address for the record."

I gave both. He nodded. I could feel the line of people behind me, just out of sight, waiting for their four minutes and fifty-seven seconds, their four minutes and twelve, their three-thirty.

I looked up and found a few faces I recognized. Some Commissioners wore the polite interest of people resigned to a long afternoon. Some had the gentle smirk they save for someone who's going to be "colorful" but not consequential. One looked tired enough to cry.

"I'm gonna read a poem," I said. "Hope that's okay."

The smirks brightened. The tired one blinked awake.

"Please proceed," the Chair said, in that careful tone bureaucrats use when they sense something unscheduled coming.

My remarks began with descriptions of the first shift and the second, the graveyard and the weekend side hustle. I said the job names like gospel: janitors, cashiers, bus drivers, nurses, men with calloused hands and women who cleaned up after the ones making policy. The people Becky and I knew, the ones we were representing on this Thursday afternoon.

You could feel the temperature drop in the chamber. The Commissioners stiffened. The Chair looked down at his agenda packet like the words might crawl off the page and bite him. Another tapped her pen and fidgeted with her big, East Tennessee hair, counting minutes.

But the poem didn't care about minutes. It was a shot across the bow of Knoxville privilege—five pages of hard truth about who gets to speak at three-thirty on a weekday and who's too busy keeping the lights on.

When the timer on the wall hit ninety seconds, I was hitting my stride. The poem turned sharp, calling out the hollow civility of meetings like this one, where "community input" meant the same ten faces who could afford to show up. Someone coughed near the back, nervous and loud, like a starter pistol in church.

At zero, the timer flashed red. The Chair lifted his hand.

I kept reading.

"Sir," he said, carefully, "your time—"

I looked up. "Are you cutting me off?"

The room made a small sound—half amusement, half warning. The Chair glanced toward the city attorney. The attorney didn't move.

"Please conclude," the Chair said. "Quickly."

I continued. Softer now. I let the poem breathe. I put my hand on the paper like it might try to fly away. I watched the Chair try another look at the lawyer and the lawyer shake his head softly: you're stuck now. Sometimes the rules are funny that way. Once you invite the citizens to speak, you cannot un-invite the language.

Becky had asked for time. I gave it to her.

During public comment, people often step out into the hallway. Phones come out. Faces change. You don't need to know who's calling whom to see that the temperature is moving. I let my eyes drift just over the top of the dais, to the glass beyond the room where the city hung blue and ordinary. Inside, the Commissioners looked at one another and whispered numbers with their eyebrows. You can count votes in silence if you're practiced.

A few more pages in, I felt the poem shift again—out of the direct ask, into something that sounded like a benediction if you squinted. It said, "Look at the map in your head." It said, "How many times have we asked one neighborhood to shoulder the burden for the rest." It did not say redlining or poverty, but everyone on that stage knew exactly what I meant. Sometimes the word shuts the door before the idea can get a foot in.

It said, "The kids here deserve a simpler walk home. Not one past guns and trouble. Not anymore."

"Sir," the Chair tried again, voice rising to the pitch you save for a toddler at the edge of a decorative fountain. "If you could—"

"Oh come on. I'll be done…soon," I smiled at him, trying to take the sting out.

Someone behind me clapped once, immediately embarrassed by their own hands. Others followed.

"Let him finish," they began to chant.

I finished the poem at the same pace I'd started—no triumphant rise, no voice like a courtroom drama.

"Thank you," I said, and meant it.

The Chair exhaled. "Thank you," he said. "Next speaker."

I folded the pages, left them on the lectern on purpose, and returned to my seat. The developer's man made a note with a pen that didn't touch the paper. The neighborhood liaison squeezed my shoulder hard enough to leave a thumbprint.

"Nice," she said. "Who wrote it?"

"A friend," I said. "No idea where she got it. Don't shoot the messenger."

We all knew which friend.

Here's the part where memory and politics share a face. While I read, the room changed. Doors opened. Phones appeared. People who had been still suddenly had somewhere else to be. Becky didn't need a seat at the table to help rearrange it. She didn't ask me to be any part of that. She just asked me to read her damn poem.

When the Chair called for the vote, the smiles around the horseshoe gave the ending away. In certain rooms, you can read the roll call before it's spoken; it plays across faces like weather.

"Motion fails," the Chair said.

The developer's man blinked, as if the script supervisor had changed the ending without telling him. The neighborhood row didn't cheer. People think you cheer. You don't. You breathe. You pick up your purse and your binder and your kid. You go home to the same street and you sleep a little easier until the next docket grows teeth and puts its target on your block, and you keep going because that's what neighborhoods do.

The article the next day was a small rectangle of type that would slip through a thousand kitchens and become a refrigerator magnet in one of them. It said that for the first time in memory, the Metropolitan Planning Commission had been poetry slammed. My name sat there in print like a thumbtack. Becky's did not.

If you didn't know, you wouldn't know.

If you knew, you smiled.

I think of that afternoon whenever somebody tells me East Knoxville is a charity case—a ward of better zip codes, waiting on a rescue that shows up with a clipboard and a camera. That corridor didn't get $10 million because a rich person woke up generous one day. It got it because citizens like Becky carried folding chairs into rooms and stayed. It got it because neighborhood associations learned to write in the language of patience and then speak in the language of alarm when they had to. It got it because people like Becky built quiet bridges between folks who couldn't stand one another but could be made to stand next to one another for five minutes, which is sometimes long enough to move a vote.

The project didn't die because a poem out-argued a plan. It died because a poem bought the one thing power hates to give up—time—and Becky spent that currency perfectly.

We used to say we'd turn Park City into a calendar. We didn't need to. Park City turned into a witness. Every porch that looks out on the streets parallel and perpendicular to Magnolia Avenue remembers the old way—how long people called it hopeless, how much easier it was to blame a neighborhood than to admit a city had been shunting its troubles east since the first maps of segregation.

I have the clipping somewhere, but I don't need to see it. If I close my eyes, I can still hear Becky's voice on the phone the night before, pleased with her own audacity.

"Whatever they do," she said, "you keep reading."

The next time I saw her, we didn't talk about it much. That was our way. She'd ask if I was eating, and if I wasn't, she'd drive us over to Chandler's Deli for some bone-sucking barbeque, collards, and cornbread. She'd say how tired Magnolia looked that week and how you could tell the planners weren't walking it because they kept saying "activation" like people were a switch. We'd trade neighborhood gossip and decide which parts were useful and which parts were just noise with shoes.

"Do you still have the poem?" I asked her once.

She tilted her head, mischievous.

"Maybe," she said.

Which meant yes. It also meant it wasn't leaving her house.

"What would you have done if they'd cut the mic?" I asked.

"They weren't going to cut the mic," she said. "But if they had, you were going to keep reading. Nice and loud."

"You didn't tell me that part."

"You didn't need it," she said, sipping her tea. "You already knew you would."

I wanted to ask how many calls it took, how many favors she named, how many near-misses kept huffing and puffing on the other end of the line while I was reciting the section about night-shift sleep. I wanted a diagram of the vote like a coach's whiteboard, a play-by-play with arrows. But that would have cheapened the best thing about her. She didn't turn her work into legend because legends stop being useful. She preferred usefulness.

We stood up to leave and she checked the time, eyes narrowing like she was reading cloud cover before a storm.

"Got to go," she said. "Somebody I love is about to do something dumb."

"That narrows it down to the entire city," I said.

"Exactly," she said, and smiled.

Years later, when people asked what Becky French Brewer was like, I never started with politics. I started with the way she saw holes in things. Not the cynical kind—the structural kind. The patterns. She could look at a plan and find the seam where the next bad decision would get in. She could close it with three phone calls and a flurry of sticky notes that made sense only to her. She could spot the one sentence in a planning document that meant "yes" when the speaker thought it meant "maybe". She could hear the wiggle room in a city lawyer's voice. She could force a decision that wasn't ready, and delay a decision that was too ready, both in the service of a neighborhood that just wanted to keep breathing.

She loved Knoxville like a mechanic loves an old engine: aware of the noises, wary of the leaks, unwilling to junk it. She never wanted the hood ornament. She wanted clean fuel lines and a steady idle. She wanted the car to make it across Magnolia without stalling.

"Becky," I asked her one time, "why do you love Knoxville so much?"

"It's simple, Doug," she chuckled. "This is where I keep my shit."

I didn't write the poem. I carried it for her. I would do it again in a heartbeat.

I'm not sentimental about city government. They'll eat your heart, ask for your parking stub, and refuse to validate. But there are moments—brief as sparrows—when a room built for compliance turns into a stage for plain, honest speech. That MPC day was one.

The poem wasn't elegant. It wasn't supposed to be. It did the thing poetry used to do before people started apologizing for it in classrooms: it said something simple in a way that made simple sound like truth.

People still ask if it really happened—if a room built to manage citizens let one of them take his time. I tell them the truth: sometimes bureaucracy chooses patience because it's cheaper than a scene.

The first copy of Becky's poem stayed on the lectern. The second came home with me. The timer kept blinking either way.

## Three
# LAST CHRISTMAS IN HOLSTON HILLS

This tale begins on Andie Ray's front porch on East Oklahoma Avenue, where the air smelled faintly of honeysuckle. Andie wore a bright floral sundress—and a broad straw hat that looked like she'd stepped out of a Frances Hodgson Burnett novel.

Burnett, and historic preservation, were two of Andie's obsessions. She turned both into a practice—running Vagabondia, her dress shop on Market Square, named for Burnett's river-bluff home, and treating Knoxville like an old novel that could still be read if you paid attention.

Andie also worked for a downtown law firm and was on the board of a number of nonprofits.

But that afternoon, we weren't talking about a 19th-century English novelist, or the children's books that later made her famous. Burnett was a reference point—an earlier version of someone learning how to read a place. What interested Andie was that Knoxville version: poor, but watchful, living above the river bluffs near downtown, surviving by noticing what other people passed over.

"I still can't get over it," Andie said, cradling a glass of iced tea with a lemon slice afloat. "You know what that librarian told me?"

Becky and I leaned in—we'd heard the story, but Andie told it like she was re-living the moment, and it hit fresh every time.

"She looked right at me," Andie said, "and said, 'Your grandfather killed my grandfather.' Just like that. No warning. I thought she was joking."

But she wasn't. The librarian had been tracing her own family line—and somewhere in the tangle of Joneses, Howards, and McGhees, bloodlines had crossed with gunfire.

"That's Knoxville for you," Andie said with a stunned little laugh. "You start out researching genealogy and end up apologizing for the dead."

We were there that afternoon to go over Becky's notes—her latest find on the Holston Hills triple murder of 1929. Becky could unearth what everyone else had chosen to forget. Her folders were stacked in neat piles—yellowed, dog-eared, and heavy with what people prefer not to say out loud.

The victims: Dr. Barclay Jones, a physician; Lucy Lane Jones, his wife; and her fourteen-year-old nephew, George Lane. Christmas Day. The house ransacked, Dr. Jones's pockets turned out, but Lucy's pearls still clasped around her throat—the detail that haunted Becky.

"Doesn't make sense," she said, sipping tea. "If it was robbery, why leave the jewelry?"

"Because it wasn't robbery," Andie said, tilting her hat back. "It was theatre. Someone wanted it to look like robbery."

Andie wasn't a mountain-porch storyteller. She was downtown Knoxville bohemia—part law-firm fixer, part archivist, part boutique owner.

Becky slid out three photocopies of the New York Times dated December 25, 1929 and passed them to us like a case file.

"Here," she said. "Read this: 'Man, Wife and Boy Slain in Tennessee: Knoxville Doctor and Kin Are Found Beaten to Death in Their Home.'"

People talked about those killings like they happened in another century, but it was modern Knoxville. Garages. Telephones on the wall in a hallway alcove. Hedge trimmers, golf-course plats. And the brutality was not gunfire; the victims were bludgeoned to death.

"They found the doctor first," I read. "In the garage. Skull crushed. His hat still in the car. Hedge shears nearby. An axe. Pockets pulled inside-out, gold watch missing. Blood in the snow where he fought back."

"Inside," Becky added, "Lucy and George in the basement. Her clothes torn. Bruises up and down her arms and legs. Telephone ripped from the wall and left in the middle of the room. But the diamond rings and wristwatch—untouched."

She read from the column: "Officials differ on the motive, some believing assault, others robbery."

"That difference," I said, "is 1929 Tennessee: the coroner saw theft; the sheriff saw sex."

"And both saw convenience," Andie added. "A servant, newly hired, Black. That's all they needed."

They meant J. T. (Jim) Harris, hired just before Christmas. The Times called him "a negro employed a week or ten days ago." Sheriff Walker Anderson leaned toward "assault." Even on paper, it read like prejudice dressed as evidence.

Becky knew better. She'd pulled his marriage record from her folder without ceremony—Jim Harris and his new wife, Mattie, married only days before the murders. "He was twenty-six," she said. "Worked steady. Had a place on Vine Avenue. You don't start a marriage by killing your employer's family on Christmas Day."

"You already checked the city directories, Becky," I grinned. She just chuckled. She was ready to present her case.

The official story didn't care about motive; it cared about comfort. Knoxville's white public needed the murders to fit a narrative they already trusted—the same one that had justified the 1919 Gay Street riot, when white mobs torched Black-owned businesses after a rumor that a Black man had insulted a white woman. No assault was proven then, either. But it didn't matter. The rumor was enough to summon rifles, fires, and fear that still hadn't cooled ten years later.

"They never proved assault," I said. "Only that Mrs. Jones screamed. The rest was projection—white panic dressed up as chivalry."

"Robbery felt common," Becky said. "Assault on a woman made it righteous rage and moral panic."

"And both made it simple," Andie added. "And convenient. You hang a Black man and call it justice instead of hysteria."

When they caught Harris, he didn't run far—just hid at a cousin's place in Mechanicsville, hoping to clear his name. They tried him in a single day. No physical evidence, no witness, just the badge and the mood of the city. The paper praised the "efficiency of Southern justice." He was sent to Nashville, to the electric chair at the state penitentiary, and on January 22, 1931, he was executed.

Becky had found his final statement in a yellowed News-Sentinel clipping: "I didn't kill nobody," he said. "The Lord knows I didn't."

For a moment the porch went quiet, and nobody reached for another page. In 1931, Knoxville had its new golf courses but no integrated schools, new trolley lines but segregated hospitals. White civility had always been the city's preferred language.

The porch fan kept turning. Knoxville liked to think of itself as stable—doctors, banks, committees—while the Depression already nipped the edges: banks shuttering on Magnolia, men sleeping in boxcars near the railyards.

We dug deeper into Becky's case file.

Harris vanished and became a headline: NEGRO SERVANT SOUGHT. Within two days, he was the only theory anyone repeated. When they found him, what he said didn't matter. The verdict was already waiting.

"He said he was innocent?" Andie asked.

"Right up to the end," I nodded as we each leafed through the records.

We let the silence do its work. The article's phrases echoed—mutilated bodies...Negro servant sought...motive uncertain. No mention of grief. No room for doubt.

"You know what bugs me most?" Andie said, folding the clipping along its brittle seams. "The brutality. The rage."

"Maybe it was something else? Revenge, maybe? An old debt?"

"Some families never stopped settling scores," Andie said. "They just learned to do it indoors."

Becky and I nodded. We all kept coming back to the last name: Jones. A common name, perhaps, but not in Andie's view.

I opened my laptop and started digging into Ancestry.com, and quickly created a Jones family tree. Together, we worked backward, Andie and Becky looking over my shoulder as we dug deeper. In 1910, Lucy and Dr. Barclay Joshua Jones lived at Gill and Irwin Streets in Old North with Lucy's parents, Buffalow and Frances Ransom.

Barclay's parents were Dr. Charles Calhoun Jones and his wife, Margaret White McGhee of Madisonville in Monroe County.

We froze because Becky and I already knew what Andie had been working on.

She'd been tracing the Jones–McGhee–Howard feud for months, quietly, without selling it as a theory. Andie didn't speculate first. She documented. Names. Dates. Court records. Marriages. Indictments. She was interested in how violence survives respectability—not how it announces itself.

She'd shown us the early material before: Monroe County headlines that kept recycling the same surnames, the same disputes, the same witnesses switching sides. Violence that moved with the people who could afford to move.

So when Margaret White McGhee appeared next to Charles Calhoun Jones on my screen, it didn't feel like a coincidence.

It felt like confirmation.

"If this really was the last act in that feud," I said, "no one would admit it. By '29, Knoxville was selling itself as modern. Feuds were 'mountain folklore,' not something that happened east of the country club."

"Appearances are this city's currency," Andie said. "Always have been."

Becky didn't comment. She just reached back into her folder, already moving on to the next document, because once the pattern shows itself, the work stops being interpretive.

"The Joneses were murdered," Andie observed. "Harris was executed, and the neighborhood still advertises peace like nothing happened."

Becky tapped the line about Lucy's pearls—still clasped, still there. "They didn't take what mattered," she said. "They staged what they wanted people to believe."

Andie shook her head. "This city doesn't kill the past," she said. "It repackages it."

"Ghosts?" I asked.

"More like reputation," she said.

Our porch conversation continued into the evening, moving through Andie's genealogy notes—names repeating across decades: Jones, McGhee, Howard. Deeds. Marriages. Court records. The same families intersecting again and again.

The implication was clear, even if no one said it outright. Knoxville has never liked the word "feud". It prefers cleaner explanations—isolated incidents, unfortunate events, bad individuals. Politeness makes things easier to file away.

But the violence in Holston Hills didn't read as random. It was beginning to read as settled business—methodical, personal, and final.

• • •

We met again a few nights later, with rain on the sidewalks and wet coats on Andie's chair. Andie had her binders open, Sweetwater Telephone clippings flattened beneath plastic sleeves.

"Start where it actually starts," I said. "Monroe County. No rumor. Just records."

"It's worse on paper," Andie said. "Because you can't argue with it."

January 1900: MCGHEES ACQUITTED.

John B. McGhee and his son Joe tried for the murder of Ernest Howard. Not guilty.

The state's witnesses were Tom Howard and his wife, Alva—who also happened to be John McGhee's daughter and Joe's sister. In the first trial, Alva testified for her husband. In the second, she recanted, said Tom had forced her to lie. The grand jury answered with fifteen counts of perjury—the longest indictment in county history. She filed for divorce and moved back in with her father.

"That's where it stops being abstract," Andie said. "Tom Howard was my great-great-great-grandfather."

The feud didn't end. It kept going.

September 1900: DESPERATE DUEL.

The Clue Hotel in Madisonville erupted—twenty-five shots fired. Dr. Charles Calhoun Jones dead within the hour. Josh Jones and Calvin Howard mortally wounded. Tom Howard present. Unharmed.

March 1902: TOM HOWARD KILLED—SHOT DOWN IN KNOXVILLE YESTERDAY BY JOSH AND MOULTRIE JONES.

They followed him from the Gay Street Bridge into the 100 block near Jackson Avenue. Ten shots. Six or seven into Tom. Witnesses heard Joshua Jones say, "That's enough. We've got him."

The Jones brothers walked into the Knoxville Banking Company, posted $20,000 bond, and went home. No conviction that held. The public record ends there.

I said, "So a Howard is murdered downtown in 1902. And twenty-seven years later, a Jones household is wiped out in Holston Hills."

"Same families," Andie said. "Different zip code."

"And your family is on both sides of this," Becky added quietly.

"Exactly," Andie said. "By 1929, the Joneses weren't feud people anymore. They were professionals. Doctors. Civic names. You can't be a founding family and a feud family at the same time. One story had to disappear."

"Bloodlines got rebranded," I said.

"They turned violence into respectability," Andie replied. "And when the past resurfaced, it needed a substitute."

I thought of Gay Street in 1902—ten shots in public, witnesses everywhere—and Holston Hills in 1929, sealed rooms and controlled narratives.

It didn't stop. It just got better at hiding.

We sat with the pages and the names.

Andie shook her head. "No—they killed stories too. They made sure the record stopped where it was convenient."

Andie reached for the binder, then let her hand fall.

"That's a body count of like…nine," she said quietly. "Plus or minus three, if you count that last Christmas in Holston Hills."

"I do," I said.

"I do too," Becky added. "Can't prove it yet, but makes a helluva lot more sense than Jim Harris."

"What matters isn't the number," Andie said. "It's the pattern."

We listened to the rain ease up, and nobody pretended the body count wasn't real.

We knew we had much more digging to do. To understand why those names kept resurfacing, we had to leave Knoxville and go back to where the records begin.

### Epilogue—The Short Straw

My friends Andie and Becky are both gone now. Andie, suddenly and unexpectedly in 2015 after a short illness, followed by Becky in 2017 after her cancer returned. Both gone too soon, both leaving silences I still notice. Some evenings I still catch myself thinking of iced tea and front porch stories, or the rustle of Becky's nicotine-stained folders as she lays out another century of secrets on the table.

We've each been keepers of questions. I happen to be stubborn enough to stay behind and turn questions into plausible stories—if not neat answers—hoping others will continue to carry the torch for stories like these.

Andie used to say Knoxville would never tell its own story truthfully until someone wrote it down without flinching. Becky believed the same thing, and both of them worked with proof instead of faith—deeds, indictments, brittle newspaper clippings that came apart at the folds. Between them they built the scaffolding. I've filled in the spaces.

The tea gone stale, the files now stacked in my studio. Rain on the roof. Knoxville keeps its stories alive—the gentry, the dreamers, the guilty and the good—all walking the same brick streets pretending history is behind them.

But sometimes the city lets a secret through.

A few years after Andie died, Zoo Knoxville announced the birth of a baby gorilla—a girl, named "Andie." The name was chosen to honor Andie Ray, who had championed the zoo's work to save Western lowland gorillas from extinction. Andie had connected her family to that effort, naming the zoo's first newborn gorilla Obi, or "heart." The name Andie means "brave, strong, valiant, and courageous."

## Four
# THE JONES-MCGHEE-HOWARD FEUD

Andie, Becky and I dug deeper into the record in the months that followed. At first the disputes looked ordinary: property lines, business arrangements, personal grudges. But when the documents were laid side by side, the pattern changed. These were not isolated disagreements. They were sustained, overlapping conflicts that moved through families, institutions, and time.

Andie went back to her family, many amateur historians, and asked more questions. Becky dug deeper into the public record. We started confirming more details the official records and news accounts had avoided. What follows is what we were able to piece together over the following months.

• • •

**March 20, 1902.** On the southwest corner of Knoxville's Jackson Avenue and Gay Street, a signboard creaks under a mild wind: Whitesides & Keener—Shooting Gallery, Refreshments.

Inside, lamps burn oily and low. The ceiling is tin, pressed with patterns that make bullets reverberate when they miss. Three lanes run like alleys to a painted backstop—stags, concentric circles, a mustached outlaw grinning from behind his kerchief. The floor is sawdust, indifferent to spit and tobacco juice. A piano near the front picks out a ragged tune for two men who aren't listening.

Tom Howard has the bar at his back. By then he was already a feud survivor, but he was also a Knoxville grocer over on Crooked Street near West Fifth—a man who had come down from Monroe County, chasing the narrow but real opportunities of a growing city, selling flour and coffee to people who no longer knew his name. He had a wife tied to the McGhee name, and the papers never missed a chance to remind readers of it: John McGhee's daughter. Joe McGhee's sister.

He's tall, coat unbuttoned, hat tipped back. Some said he had a badge—others said he borrowed it when he wanted a discount on whiskey. His right hand rests near the butt of a revolver he hasn't drawn in two years and won't get to holster again.

The door opens. The room's noise recalculates.

Joshua R. Jones—jaw set, hair silvering at the edges—steps in first, followed by his nephew Moultrie, leaner and younger, with the cockiness of a man practiced in ignoring good judgment. They do not remove their hats. The bartender looks from one to the other and then at his bottles, as if he might need them for cover.

A single drinker laughs from habit and stops when nobody follows him.

Tom turns from the bar, his reflection briefly splitting over the mirror's scratches. He doesn't move his feet. He lets his eyes do the traveling.

"Boys," he says, voice conversational, as if this were a quarrel over a deck of cards. "We settled this already."

Josh answers without shifting his weight. "Not proper."

Moultrie: "We ain't finished."

The piano clinks its way to silence. A lane boy, twelve if he's a day, freezes with a target reel in his hands. Somebody in the back coughs the way people do before they run.

No one will later agree who fired the first shot—whether it came from the left or the right, whether a hand shook or a nerve misread the world. But once the sound happens, time stops: a flash against a whiskey bottle, a gasp that never finishes.

Then everything happens at once.

Howard's shoulder kicks. Glass detonates into cold rain. A mirror throws a copy of the room to the floor. A second shot, a third, and then the arithmetic of hatred accelerates—thirty shots in under a minute, the sound stacking until the ear can't tell the difference between pistol and echo. Bullets chew plaster, nick tin, punch sawdust into smoke.

Tom Howard works his revolver the way a man bails water—quick, efficient, doomed. He angles toward the lanes, trying for the depth of the room, but the backstop offers only paint and finality. A round takes the hat from his head. Another stitches the hem of his coat. He pivots, slips in the sawdust, recovers, and in that scrap of balance loses the second he most needs.

A bullet finds him under the ribs. It enters so clean he looks surprised. Another hits high in the shoulder and spins him into the lane rail. He takes a step forward and sits hard against the backstop, his breath leaving him.

The Joneses keep their formation—uncle a half-step forward, nephew a fraction left—firing methodically until the logic of the moment empties both pistols. No shouting, no flourish. The practiced silence of men who have rehearsed this in their heads for weeks.

The bartender stays crouched, cursing the alphabet of glass and spilled whiskey at his feet. The lane boy finally remembers to breathe. A bottle still intact.

Gunsmoke drifts in torn ribbons to the ceiling fan that hasn't worked right since winter.

On the floor, Tom Howard tries to stand and cannot. His hand is still on the revolver but there's no argument left in it. He looks toward the door like a man remembering the distance to the river. Somewhere in him is a bullet from another year—Citico, a rifle ball to the head that he survived despite every story wishing otherwise. He has never believed in odds. He believes in staying put.

That belief does not save him.

By the time the sound collapses into itself, the room has already decided how to forget. Someone mutters a prayer. Someone else counts holes in the tin. The piano offers a single accidental chord and quits.

Josh breaks the spell by reloading with a patience that makes other men uncomfortable. He closes the cylinder, pockets one extra round, and nods once to the bartender—thanks for the hospitality. Moultrie snaps his pistol shut, surveys the floor with an expression you could mistake for boredom if you didn't know him. They holster in unison, a choreography learned from necessity, not theater.

They walk out together into clean daylight.

On Gay Street, the air feels innocent. Wagons rattle past; a woman steps from a milliner's in a sunny hat with no connection to what's just happened. The Joneses turn south on Gay Street, not hurrying, eyes forward, the city blessing their calm with room to pass. Two blocks is not far unless you've just emptied a century into a minute.

They reach the Knoxville Banking Company and step through the door as if opening an account. The clerk behind the polished counter looks up, then down, then up again, his mouth choosing a posture. Josh sets his pistol on the marble, Moultrie follows with his, the metal small and suddenly uninteresting in a room built to make money feel holy.

"We're here to surrender," Josh says.

The clerk will later tell it three ways to anyone who buys him a pint, but the part he won't change is that he felt relief before fear—that something inevitable had finally found its correct desk. He takes the pistols with thumb and forefinger, as if they might smudge the ledger.

Back at the shooting gallery, someone is running for a man with a stretcher. Howard is still breathing but not for long. The sawdust is thick with his blood. The boy puts a hand to the outlaw painted at the back, as if the figure might offer help.

By sundown, the presses finish their work and the newsboys go shouting into the streets. The headline is the kind that claims both certainty and innocence: KNOXVILLE HAS BLOODY TRAGEDY—TOM HOWARD KILLED BY TWO JONES BROTHERS—RESULT OF AN ANCIENT FEUD.

That Tom, the dead man, was a Knoxville policeman appeared in some headlines and vanished in others, depending on how badly the press needed the word "feud" to do the moral laundering. They move the facts into a drawer labeled Heritage, a place where the violent become provincial and the dead become educational. Neighbors read it aloud at supper along with the weather forecast. Down in Madisonville, a lawyer folds the paper, stares at the hills, and thinks about a train to Knoxville.

Night comes to Gay Street the way it always does—light by light, window by window. Men wash the blood from the gallery and call it business. They'll be open tomorrow. Business will be strong with the new dents in the tin ceiling.

On the bank's marble counter, the clerk has set the pistols side by side—two small instruments resting where money once decided futures. He straightens them until they mirror each other and pauses.

The city will not forget, but it will organize its memory quickly.

In the morning, the story will already be older than the men in it, the headline having done its efficient work. By the time the train leaves for Monroe County with Josh and Moultrie Jones on it, the shot that started it will belong to whatever version makes the teller virtuous. The rest will be filed under that phrase the paper loves—the phrase that puts a lace collar on catastrophe and teaches it to sit up straight: RESULT OF AN ANCIENT FEUD.

East Tennessee papers were good at turning blood into myth—especially when myth sold better than accountability. Before Gay Street made this feud a headline, Monroe County had already made it a template.

• • •

Andie leaned forward, elbows on her knees, her mug cooling between her palms. The porch had gone quiet except for one of the cats prowling the rail like a small, impatient ghost.

"So that's how it ends," she said. "The last official death in the feud. My great-great-great-grandfather, Tom Howard."

I nodded. "Ends, or reboots?"

"Hard to tell," she said. "Let's go back to the beginning."

It began in Monroe County in November 1893—a wedding day the neighbors whispered about before it happened.

Thomas Calloway Howard, nineteen, son of a farming family known for pride and work, married Alva McGhee—thirteen—daughter of John B. McGhee. The papers would later lean on her age the way a prosecutor leans on a jury: not as context, but as a weapon.

The McGhees were courthouse people—tax records, banknotes, deeds folded in desk drawers that carried the future of every family in the county. The Howards were farmers, stubborn and sunburned, their worth counted in acres they could plow and debts they refused to owe.

The marriage wasn't a union; it was an act of defiance.

John McGhee forbade it. His daughter obeyed her heart instead, and that was the first gun drawn, even if it fired no bullet. She slipped away with Tom to a justice of the peace in Madisonville who didn't ask questions.

It didn't stay quiet. One Chattanooga paper ran it like a manhunt—armed kin riding after them with Winchesters and pistols, the county treating a child bride and an elopement like a public emergency. Whatever love they claimed, whatever defiance they meant, the outside world read the same thing: property in motion. The record shows the date and their names in precise clerk's script—nothing about the shouting that followed, or how the clerk kept his head down while the ink dried.

By evening, the courthouse square buzzed with gossip disguised as moral concern.

"She's just a girl."

"He's just a Howard."

"Her daddy'll skin him alive."

Knoxville papers gave it a single column inch—ELOPEMENT IN MONROE COUNTY—but in small towns, an inch is enough room for a century.

John McGhee didn't come to the wedding. He did, however, send word: "If the boy steps on my land again, he'll leave by horse or coffin."

Tom Howard stepped on it anyway.

He brought Alva home to a small house off the Citico Road—two rooms, a fireplace, the beginnings of a life that neither money nor permission could grant. Neighbors said the young bride hung curtains herself, embroidered with flowers she'd never seen. They said she was sweet to everyone but her father and loyal to everyone else. They said Tom was good to her when he wasn't busy proving something to the rest of the county.

For a while, there was an uneasy peace. McGhee pretended the marriage hadn't happened; Howard pretended forgiveness was unnecessary. But the hills remember better than people do. When John McGhee passed Tom's fence line on horseback, he stared straight ahead. When Tom saw McGhee at church, he stood outside until the service was over. Each silence was a fuse waiting for the right match.

What turned feud into destiny was the Jones connection.

John's sister Margaret McGhee had married Dr. Charles Calhoun Jones, a respected man of education, violinist, Confederate veteran, and another justice of the peace. The Jones name carried its own authority in the county, and through Margaret, they stood shoulder to shoulder with the McGhees. What began as a family argument now had enough names, property, and pride to qualify as history.

From that day forward, the county drew invisible lines between the three families.

On one side: McGhees and Joneses, with their records and courthouse keys.

On the other: Howards, with their calloused hands and stubborn memory.

In between stood the women—Alva, Margaret, and Sarah—each carrying the burden of keeping the peace in powder-keg households.

Tom and Alva's marriage license became a declaration—love signed in ink, defiance notarized by the state of Tennessee.

Andie closed her eyes and finished the thought.

"It's funny," she said. "They wrote their names together once, and the rest of us have been rewriting them ever since."

Somewhere between that November wedding and the gunfire nine years later on Gay Street, a family argument turned biblical.

• • •

**March, 1898.** Five years after the wedding, the feud had gone from family matter to county entertainment, whispered in the courthouse corridors and printed in the Sweetwater Telephone with all the decorum of gossip dressed in its Sunday best. By 1898, no one remembered the vows—only the class warfare that followed.

One morning, Tom's brothers Henry and Ernest Howard rode out from their father's farm with Jim Murr, a cousin on their mother's side. The sun was new, the ground still slick with rain. They carried no warrants, no letters—just a warning. Word had reached them that John B. McGhee, still enraged that his daughter had married beneath her, was busy making threats again.

"Pa's fixing to take a rifle to Tom," Henry said, reining up at the ridge. "Heard it myself from the postmaster's boy."

Murr spat into the mud. "Then we'd best get to him first."

Their horses cut through the Citico Valley—Overhill Cherokee country, where Scots-Irish men had married Cherokee women for generations.

The Howard brothers and their cousin Jim passed the McGhee place on the way to Tom's—a quarter mile of distance and a century of pride. The windows were shuttered though it was daylight. No one waved from the porch.

When they reached Tom's cabin, Alva was outside hanging laundry, the white cloth snapping in the wind. Tom met them at the gate, bareheaded, sleeves rolled, a look on his face that said he'd already heard enough of every story.

"Pa's been talking," Henry told him. "You best stay clear of his fence line."

Tom shook his head. "We're all square now. I got no quarrel left with him."

"Funny," Ernest said. "He says different."

But Tom wouldn't be drawn. "He's my wife's father. That's a burden I'll have to carry."

They shared a quick meal—biscuits and cold ham—and when the talk ran dry, the three men mounted up again to head home, the horses turning back down the same road they'd come.

They never made it past the McGhee place.

Witnesses said John McGhee and his son Joe came running from behind the rail fence, guns already up. John carried a double-barrel shotgun, Joe a Winchester repeating rifle. No words were spoken. The first blast hit Henry Howard square in the chest, knocking him clean off his horse. The second tore through Ernest's shoulder, and before he could fall, the rifle cracked—three, four times—cutting through dust and shouts and hooves. Jim Murr tried to wheel his horse for cover, but the animal stumbled in the ditch and threw him straight into the rifle's line.

From the house, Alva heard the shots and came running. She later said it was like hearing her name spelled in gunfire. Tom was right behind her, revolver in hand, but before he reached the gate, a bullet from Joe's rifle found him just above the temple—a glancing wound that should have killed him but didn't.

He fell hard, bleeding into the clay, the revolver sliding from his grip. Alva knelt beside him, pressing her apron to the wound, praying to a God she wasn't sure was listening. Tom's eyes fluttered open, and he whispered something she never repeated. The blood kept coming. Behind them, the smoke thinned, the shouting stopped, and the McGhees went back into their house.

By dusk, word had reached Madisonville: three men dead, Tom not expected to live.

Neighbors came from every hollow to help dig the graves—Henry, Ernest, and Jim Murr, laid side by side in the same small plot, the headstones cut by hand and the names carved in rough letters that looked more like wounds than words. The preacher said they died as "defenders of kin," which is how East Tennessee grants sainthood.

Tom did survive, against expectation and maybe even preference. The doctors said the bullet had grazed the skull and taken part of his hearing with it. He spent weeks in bed, Alva tending him with hands that trembled. When he could stand again, he walked to town and swore out a complaint against her father and brother.

The trial made headlines from Sweetwater to Knoxville. The courtroom overflowed with neighbors who came to watch the county split itself in half. Alva took the stand and, with her voice shaking but clear, testified that her husband had done nothing to provoke the attack.

She said the shooting was "without cause."

She said her father had "spoken of hate as if it were an heirloom."

The papers printed her words like a confession.

Then came the rumors—always the rumors. Some claimed Ernest Howard had been paying visits to another McGhee daughter, a flirtation that turned grievance into ammunition. Others said John McGhee had seen it as one more insult, another Howard reaching above his station. Nothing was proven, but rumor doesn't need proof when it sounds familiar enough to be true.

In January 1900, after two years of postponements and courthouse politics, the McGhees were tried for murder. They smiled for the Sweetwater Telephone correspondent, shook hands with their attorney, and walked out free men. The Howards went home to an emptier table. Tom limped now; the scar above his temple caught the light when he turned his head. He said little in public. Those who saw him in town said he looked like a man who'd begun to measure his own mortality.

Three men buried, two acquitted, and a survivor who refused to forget what happened.

• • •

The porchlight had grown dim except for the glow from Andie's phone, the blue light skating across her cheek. She scrolled through an old scan of The Sweetwater Telephone, the paper browned with time and moral superiority.

"Listen to this," she said, tapping the screen. "The most sensational domestic controversy in the county's history. They made it sound like opera."

"We prefer our sinning scored to fiddle strings," I chuckled.

Andie tilted her head. "By 1900, they'd already turned it into melodrama. Alva changed her testimony, you know. Went back under her daddy's roof."

"Recanted everything she said. Claimed she'd been misled."

"Or pressured," I nodded. "Depends which porch you were sitting on."

She read the next line from memory: "'The wife of Thomas C. Howard, having been reconciled to her people, now recants her former accusations against her father and brother.'"

The tone made it sound almost noble.

"This is about to get even uglier," I observed.

"She filed for divorce right after that," Andie said. "The papers called it mutual. Nothing mutual about a woman going home to the man who shot her husband."

Andie set the phone down beside her tea. "Tom never forgave that. He couldn't. You know what he did next?"

"I can only imagine," I replied.

She smiled slyly. "Tom married Alva's sister, Maye Lawson McGhee. Quiet little thing—never even had her picture in the paper."

"Must be love," I joked.

"Oh it was a message alright," she chuckled.

"It lasted, what, a few months?" I asked.

"Long enough for both families to lose their minds. The McGhees were humiliated—first one daughter defies the father, then the other sleeps with the enemy. And the Howards weren't exactly proud of Tom either. You can imagine the gossip—Sunday sermons rewritten as warnings."

"She filed for divorce," I said. "He married the sister. Everyone else just tried to pretend it was all over."

Andie shook her head. "It never was. The county called it 'hushed up,' but that just meant everybody talked about it quieter."

She scrolled further down the article. "Here—Sweetwater, January 25, 1900: 'The McGhee–Howard matter remains the chief topic of interest. It is said that the State's witnesses have grown divided, and the parties will meet again in court.'"

I leaned back in my chair. "The State's witnesses being husband and wife."

She laughed. "Exactly. Makes for short deliberations."

"Or long grudges," I said.

The night pressed close, and Andie let the sound of a nearby train fade before she continued. "You think Alva did it for survival?"

"I think she did it because she had nowhere else to go," I said. "Her father owned the land, her husband owned the scandal, and Tennessee owned her name."

"She lived another twelve years," Andie said quietly. "That's a long time to keep breathing after everyone's written your obituary."

"What about Tom?" I asked.

Andie's smile sharpened. "Tom didn't write letters. He kept making headlines."

She handed me a photocopy of a photograph—the kind the local paper, *The Telephone*, used to print above obituaries or indictments. Tom stood stiffly, his face half-shadowed, eyes forward. The caption beneath read simply: "Howard, of the recent Citico affair."

I studied it for a while, tracing the faint line of the scar above his temple. "He looks like a man who already knows the ending."

"He did," Andie said. "Just not the date."

We sat quietly again, the sound of the neighborhood settling into itself—the pop of someone's porch light, the low hum of a car a few streets away. The past had a way of expanding to fill the silence.

"So that's how the feud learned to survive," I said finally. "Not through bullets. Through ongoing humiliation."

Andie nodded. "Pride is one thing that never bleeds out."

"Until it does," I said.

She turned the phone toward me one last time. The final line of the Telephone article stared up from the cracked glass: "Thus ends, perhaps only for a season, the most sensational domestic controversy in the county's history."

Andie looked at me over the rim of her mug. "They were right about one thing," she said. "It was only for a season."

• • •

September 18, 1900. Courthouse week always puts a harsh light on a town.

Madisonville woke early and put on its Sunday voice: the square swept, hats brushed, benches fuller than usual.

The Clue Hotel—two stories of weathered wood with a deep porch and a reputation for keeping confidences—stood a half block from the courthouse.

Men spilled from it between dockets, smoking and talking in the soft, performative register people use when a trial involves families they know too well.

Dr. Charles Calhoun Jones was there—medical doctor, justice of the peace, jacket neat, beard trimmed for dignity's sake. He was part of the McGhee clan by marriage—husband to Margaret McGhee—and that was enough to put him in the right camp without ever having to say it aloud.

He had the stance of a man who believed in paper, signatures, and sermons; he often carried a violin case under one arm.

Upstream on the Little Tennessee River, Tom Howard had been making a different sort of preparation.

He'd found a French bulldog pup the color of tobacco and cream, curled in a wicker basket at a ferry landing. He meant to take it to his mother, who loved small things with short noses and stubborn hearts.

Tom tucked the basket under his arm and started early, riding slow so as not to frighten the dog.

He told himself he'd look in on the court docket when he got to town—just to see whether the jury had a shape that could recognize what his family had been through. He choked up at the memory of Henry, Ernest, and their cousin Jim. By late morning, the square was humming—courthouse full, porch rails crowded.

The Clue's porch held a careful collection of enemies: Joneses in traveling coats, a few McGhee cousins, and across the way, Tom's brothers Calvin and Oscar, leaning on a rail.

Josh Jones had his hat tipped against the sun, eyes narrowed. Moultrie sat on the top step with his elbows on his knees, eyes locked on the adjacent courthouse doors.

Tom started up the steps with the basket tucked in close.

The pup yawned, jaw snapping shut with a click—comic, if not for the tension humming in the air.

He stepped into the hotel's shade and put a hand to the latch. Clue Hicks, the proprietor, met him there with the smile hoteliers keep for paying customers and trouble.

"Room if you like," Hicks said, voice low. "But you'll want to know who's taking supper."

Tom glanced along the porch. Dr. Charles Jones lifted his eyes, rose in courtesy; Josh stayed seated, which was its own announcement.

Calvin shifted his weight and said nothing.

"It depends," Tom said. He meant it kind; it came out wrong.

"On what you mean by 'gentlemen.'"

A sound moved through the porch—half laugh, half warning.

The pup stirred and pressed its head into the crook of Tom's elbow, as if to remind him restraint was still an option.

"Now, sir," Charles began, "we'll have none of that."

Tom turned to him. "No offense intended. My family's to be in court with your wife's. Hard for a man to keep kind company while that's true."

Josh rose then, stretching a cramp from his leg. "Truth is truth," he said. "Company is choice."

Moultrie stood, slow and deliberate. Calvin Howard slid one heel back. His brother Oscar lifted his hat, and in that breath of civility the Clue Hotel became a battlefield.

What moved first was pride—old, aggressive, and sick of it all. Tom's head dipped—not to draw, but to steady the pup climbing free of the basket.

He tucked the dog back in the basket, murmured something like "Easy now," and in that tender second the porch rearranged itself around him.

An elbow brushed a coat. A word landed with the wrong weight.

The first shot cracked loud enough to startle the pup into a squeal.

The second came close behind, the two sounds blurring into one long, shattering note.

Somebody shouted "Tom!" and somebody else "Josh!"—until names quit being useful.

Windows blew inward; wood splinters lifted like rain; the air filled with gunpowder and echo.

Dr. Jones jerked once, twice, five times—each shot smaller, crueler.

The third took his breath; the fifth learned his center. He fell backward through the doorway, violin case skidding into the wall, eyes wide at how fast dignity can disappear.

Josh cried out and clutched his side; his hat spun into the street.

Calvin Howard dropped to one knee, three bright holes blooming through his shirt like sudden flowers.

Tom swung wide to shield the basket; someone—maybe Ollie Buell, maybe no one history kept—brought a blade and opened Tom's forearm in a quick, mean stroke.

The pup clawed higher into Tom's chest; he kept it there, even bleeding—the one thing he refused to drop.

Then quiet.

The porch groaned under the weight of smoke and shock. Windows ticked, blood found seams in the boards.

Charles Jones slid down the doorjamb, eyes tracing cracks in the ceiling plaster. Josh wheezed but kept breathing. Calvin swayed and sat. Tom stared at the cut on his arm like a man who'd broken a tool he liked.

Someone ran for the other Doctor Jones.

Standing on the Clue's porch and looking across the courthouse square, you can see where Dr. Barclay Jones's practice once stood—Charles's son, thirty-two, a physician in a town that preferred its miracles small.

He was the kind of doctor who reset a brakeman's finger before breakfast and charged him a basket of collard greens and a story.

They sent a boy with a message. Barclay Jones tore across the square and up the steps of the hotel.

He knelt by his father in the doorway, fingers at the throat where pulse betrays the truth.

"Pa," he said—not plea, recognition.

He glanced at Tom—long enough to clock the cut, long enough to register how much war remained in each man.

He opened his bag, set tools on a folded handkerchief, and tried to stop the bleeding.

Charles Jones blinked—twice, then slower. Barclay leaned close. A deputy hovered nearby, notebook ready; dying declarations are one of the law's favorite genres.

Charles breathed the name "Tom..." and the deputy later swore it amounted to: Howard began the firing.

Whether truth or duty, the words settled into the room like weather. Barclay did not look up. His instruments said everything language couldn't.

By evening, Dr. Charles Calhoun Jones was dead.

Josh lived with two holes and a practiced limp.

Calvin carried three scars for the rest of his life.

Tom kept the dog, the cut, and the certainty that the county had chosen its next chapter already.

The trial came soon enough—Madisonville never delayed a spectacle it could dress up in law.

Witnesses disagreed: some honestly, others likely bribed.

Some swore Tom Howard drew first; others swore they saw a Jones pistol flash.

The pup, most trustworthy of all, slept under Tom's chair and refused comment.

When the verdict arrived—acquittal—the relief wasn't relief at all, just noise finding a place to land.

The judge explained himself in the flat grammar of procedure; the clerk stacked papers until killing felt administrative.

The town exhaled—some with grief, some with satisfaction, most with that weary Southern compromise that passes for peace.

From then on, the Clue Hotel stopped being a building and became a chapter heading.

The boys who'd watched from the street told their sons, who told their daughters, who married into both families and blurred the pronouns until nobody could stay innocent.

Standing there now, you can almost hear the firefight—the porch boards giving back their echo: the pup's whine, the brass shells rolling, a deputy clearing his throat before pretending the story was finished.

What changed that day wasn't just a reckoning—Jones blood now joined to the feud—but the scale.

It stopped being a Madisonville sorrow and learned to be a regional myth—tragic enough for print, polite enough for Sunday retelling.

Dr. Barclay Jones closed his bag, hand on the doorframe that had watched his father's last breath.

Across the rail, Tom shifted the puppy to his good arm and met the doctor's eyes.

No words.

When a county runs out of better tools, it starts assigning roles—villain, monster, martyr, hero—until the story feels tidy enough to live with. Barclay Jones didn't necessarily fit any of these. He just started tending to Tom Howard's wounds as evening enveloped the square. The courthouse flag tangled in its own rope and freed itself.

Someone swept the porch where blood had decided its path.

The pup sneezed and slept.

∙ ∙ ∙

The bistro on the hundred block of Gay Street had once been a hardware store, back when men in hats haggled over nails and burlap instead of tapas and wine lists. Now it glowed with low Edison bulbs and the polite murmur of diners who mistake history for atmosphere.

We got a table by the window—less than half a block from where Tom Howard was killed back in 1902.

Knoxville does irony better than justice. Andie stirred her drink, condensation trailing down the glass. Becky joined late, our server handing her the glass of sweet tea we had ordered for her as she took her seat.

Through all of our research into the feud, there had been one name we'd been circling for weeks—Dr. Barclay Jones—the physician who'd tried to stitch the feud shut and wound up written into its last chapter.

"Looks like Barclay made it out of Madisonville before World War I," Becky said.

"Yeah, according to the 1910 census, Lucy and Dr. Barclay Jones lived at Gill and Irwin Streets in Old North with her parents, Buffalow and Frances Ransom," I added. "His practice was somewhere near Market Square."

"So it's likely that he had known what his brother Moultrie and their uncle Josh had planned in killing Tom in 1902," Becky said. "He still lived in Madisonville then."

"They didn't take the train to Knoxville on a whim," I said. "And you can't tell me he didn't see it coming."

Becky turned her cup slowly. "But he didn't stop it."

"Maybe he couldn't," Andie said. "Or maybe he didn't try."

Outside, the rain began—soft percussion against old bricks still standing near the site where Andie's family had lost one of their own. Around the table, we observed a moment of silence.

Andie finally exhaled. "They were all at this a long time," she said softly.

The ache of injustice landed hard on each of those families. That was the thing about feuds. Nobody calls it pride while it is happening. They call it duty. Or honor. Or memory.

Long enough, and shame learns how to pass for grace.

Knoxville was good at that. Good at keeping the past close enough to charge rent in our heads, far enough not to answer for it.

We hadn't escaped the logic.

We'd just learned how to carry it without showing the knife.

We quickly turned the conversation back toward Holston Hills, to 1929, and the final Jones murders committed under the guise of domestic peace. Dr. Barclay Jones, fifty-two, his wife, and a houseguest murdered in their home—shot and beaten before dawn.

Jim Harris, the Jones family's Black servant, was arrested within hours, convicted in record time, and electrocuted in Nashville in 1931.

The papers called it a domestic outrage. We were thinking about it more as a generational echo of violence. Maybe it was Harris. But the speed of it—the neatness—felt less like justice than the county reaching for the closest body it could name without fear of consequence.

"Barclay seemed to be one of the last men standing," Becky said, eyes on her tea. "And my guess is somebody couldn't handle that. But it's just a guess."

Andie nodded slowly. "If it was a Howard, I don't want it to be. But I'd rather know than anybody pretending they were better than the rest."

It was probably impossible to prove one way or another, and the Harris execution bothered each of us just as much. What settled between us wasn't judgment or forgiveness—only the quiet unease of something history never meant to solve.

"Every family in that triangle," I said, "had a reason to end it their own way. If Harris didn't do it, then the trick would be to figure out which kind of reason felt more like justice."

Andie remained quiet, looking past me out the window.

If you believed the courthouse whispers, suspicion scattered first toward Tom Howard's brothers—Calvin and Oscar. Both had bled in Madisonville, both had lived long enough to raise sons who learned aim before arithmetic.

Calvin, scarred at the Clue Hotel, likely never forgave the Jones name or the sheriff who let his brothers' killers ride home free.

Then there were the Howard cousins—the railmen. The next generation who inherited the feud as folklore.

Barclay Jones may have once been the calm in a storm—a man of science in a rural East Tennessee county addicted to myth—yet his death proved what every feud eventually learns: civility doesn't save you; it just delays the next shot.

And then there were the McGhees and the Joneses themselves. Families implode as often as they defend. There were likely debts and inheritances, marriages tangled in property lines.

A Jones killing a Jones wasn't unthinkable—just bad manners. Even John McGhee had once tried to kill his own son-in-law, Tom Howard in the first shooting in 1898; kin blood never guaranteed peace.

And somewhere in that tangle stood Barclay himself—doctor, son, witness, burdened with more knowledge than any man could use cleanly. He'd been the physician who dressed the wounds from 1900 and watched his father die on the Clue Hotel porch. That kind of memory curdles slow.

And then there was Jim Harris. The easiest name. The one the newspapers could print without offending anyone with money. The sheriff swore he confessed. The Knoxville Sentinel swore they'd found the Jones silver in his bag. But the neighbors remembered something else—that Harris had never left the grounds without permission, that his hands shook even when he wasn't afraid.

The trial lasted a week. The verdict took less than an hour. He went to the chair in Nashville, and the county exhaled, closing the files forever.

Plenty of white citizens felt satisfied. Some were even proud—but there can be no civic pride in a resolution like that.

"Too neat," Becky said again, softly. "Too quick."

Andie brushed a finger along the rim of her glass. "Or maybe that's just how this county cleans up after itself."

The rain thickened, drumming steady against the window. Somewhere, a siren rose and fell, like an old headline replaying its own echo.

"What we're left with," I said, "are theories."

Andie leaned in. "Then maybe that's the story. Not who did it—but who still believes they didn't."

Her voice was quiet, but it carried the weight of them all—Howards, McGhees, Joneses, and the ghost of a man named Harris who likely had no descendants left to defend him.

The three of us sat there, at the end of a very old book, watching the rain write its own footnotes across the glass.

Andie had gone quiet again, tracing circles on the table with her fingertip, as if counting ghosts.

I flipped back through my notes—the ink blurred at the edges, the way it does when a story gives up pretending to be clean. "Let's face it," I said. "We've been talking about this thing like myth. But it's not myth. It's arithmetic. Somebody always pays, and we keep forgetting to count."

Becky nodded. "Count 'em, then." So I did.

## Killed

1. **Henry Howard**—April 9, 1898—shot through the chest by John McGhee near Citico.
2. **Ernest Howard**—April 9, 1898—shot and thrown from his horse, likely by Joe McGhee.
3. **Jim Murr**—April 9, 1898—cousin to the Howards, killed in the ambush by the McGhees.
4. **Dr. Charles Calhoun Jones**—September 18, 1900—Justice of the Peace, five bullets to the chest.
5. **Tom Howard**—March 20, 1902—shot by Josh and Moultrie Jones inside Whitesides & Keener's Shooting Gallery.
6. **Dr. Barclay Jones**—1929—shot and beaten in Holston Hills.
7. **Mrs. Barclay Jones**—1929—murdered alongside her husband.
8. **George Lane**, their fourteen-year-old nephew—1929—killed in the same house.
9. **Jim Harris**—1931—executed in Nashville under suspect circumstances.

## Injured

1. **Tom Howard**—April 9, 1898—shot in the head during the Citico ambush; survived but half-deaf.
2. **Josh Jones**—September 18, 1900—wounded in the Clue Hotel fight.
3. **Calvin Howard**—September 18, 1900—shot three times at the Clue Hotel; lived to tell it badly.
4. **Tom Howard** (again)—September 18, 1900—stabbed and slashed at the Clue Hotel, survived only to die two years later on Gay Street.

Becky closed her notebook first. "Nine dead," she said, "And four who lived long enough to regret it."

Andie nodded. "Well Tom got shot, stabbed and slashed twice before they finally killed him here on Gay Street. Better double-check the math."

I triple-checked the page, the symmetry, finally shaking my head at the futility of it. "That's not a feud," I said. "That's a generational suicide pact."

No one disagreed. The rain on Gay Street kept the count for us. Andie looked up, the reflection of the streetlights trembling in her eyes. "That's madness," she said.

"From what I can tell," I said, glancing at my phone, "this body count isn't far behind the Hatfield–McCoy feud up in Kentucky—just fewer headlines."

She half-smiled. "Maybe that's a blessing in disguise."

"Or maybe it's the way East Tennessee tries to keep its secrets," I said.

Outside, Gay Street shone under the rain, the pavement darkened and honest about where it had been walked. Inside, the table between us was bare except for notebooks and glasses, the kind of evidence that doesn't point anywhere new. We hadn't solved anything. We had only traced the damage, name by name, and learned how long it can last when a place decides remembering is easier than reckoning.

Five

# DEAD MAN ON DEPOT

Becky's pickup truck reverberated down Glenwood Avenue long before I saw it from my front porch—a blue-and-silver 1982 Dodge Ram, one headlight brighter than the other, a column shifter as God intended, and the racket of a small storm stuck in second gear. She pulled straight into my front yard like it was a designated parking spot, nearly clipping a crepe myrtle in full bloom. It was a truck you drive when you don't want to be noticed.

Killing the engine, she stepped out with a cigarette already lit, her mirrored sunglasses an impenetrable wall.

We'd bought the house three years earlier, with Becky's help—a deal she'd helped us arrange against impossible odds with the same charm she used to win elections. I'm sure that was her plan all along: anchor me close enough for conversations like the one we were about to have.

The porch was wide enough for both argument and memory. We had yet to restore the faded floorboards, still painted a tired gray. The columns anchored a massive brick bungalow built in 1916—a house Becky liked to remind me was designed by an early business partner of George F. Barber, Knoxville's famous mail-order architect.

From that perch, you could see the maples across the street in front of the dilapidated Brownlow Elementary sagging under summer heat, hear the hiss of trains along the Norfolk Southern line beyond the bridge, and feel the whole neighborhood breathing. Old North Knoxville—where porches doubled as pulpits and gossip moved faster than the traffic grinding through the Glenwood Avenue cut between Fourth and Gill and Old North.

Inside, through the screen door, the staircase caught a glimmer of half-light, but out here was where truth bounced off of chipped paint, scuffed woodwork, and cracked leaded glass. It revealed itself from rocking chairs, between sips of something cold, a rolled joint, or half a pack of Marlboros.

Becky wasn't a woman who knocked. She made an entrance, hips swaying, lush silver hair blazing in the afternoon light. She wore sleeveless blouses, that let her brag without saying a word.

"If you've got good upholstery," she'd once said, "don't hide it under a tarp."

She had a laugh that could cut through humidity—half velvet, half sandpapered by years of smoke—and she arrived like she had better things to do but chose you anyway.

"Thought you were dead," I said, looking up over the edge of my laptop, pushing my bifocals back up my face.

She blew smoke sideways, grinning. "Not yet, sugar. But I got a story about one who was."

She came up the steps, kissed my cheek, and sat in my porch rocker like it was owed to her. The boards creaked.

"Lord, you look like you been editing all night," she said. "That forehead's got more tension than a city council meeting."

"Been trying to remember what's real," I said. "You here to help or make it worse?"

She laughed. "Little of both."

Becky had worked for Mayor Randy Tyree back when Knoxville still thought it might turn blue again. She'd studied Sheriff Herman Wayland like scripture and could pull more votes out of a beer joint than the entire Democratic Party office on Gay Street. Between campaigns, she kept Positively Living alive—a small AIDS-outreach nonprofit that picked up where the city looked away—charity that kept kids in shoes and drag queens in sequins.

She wasn't just clever; she was formidable—a Mensa pin somewhere in that jewelry box of hers, though she never mentioned it unless cornered by a man who mistook her accent for ignorance. She'd let him talk himself into a knot before cutting the rope with one clean line.

"You ever hear about the dead guy over on Depot Street?" she asked, leaning forward, eyes bright.

"I heard you tell it once at a party," I said. "Every time you drink Miller Lite in the daylight."

"This one's been on my mind lately." She waved her cigarette like a wand. "Jot this down for later."

She had a storyteller's posture—elbow on the chair arm, wrist cocked, cigarette balanced just so—like punctuation was optional but accuracy wasn't.

It worries me now, knowing Becky is gone, how much "later" would mean.

"It was hot, baby. I mean hot enough to fry an egg. Somewhere around '49 or '50. Depot Street—back when it was all rail yards and rough trade. Two rival funeral homes, both running ambulance service. You remember how that worked—one car, two jobs. You got there first, you got the body and the burial fee. Morbid capitalism at its finest."

I nodded, but she didn't need encouragement.

"So this poor fella drops dead behind one of those beer-and-pickled-egg joints. Heart gave out, or liver, or both. Soon as word gets out, two hearses come flying down Gay Street and take a hard right on Depot by the Regas—drag-racing for the body. Each driver swearing it's his by right of jurisdiction—whatever the hell that means. They start shouting, cussing, near come to blows right there over the corpse."

She took a long drag and exhaled slowly.

"Now, it's too hot to leave him in the street, so they drag the dead man into the bar to 'cool off.' Set him upright in a booth like he's waiting on a beer. One of the drivers even props a hat on his head. I swear it's true."

"Becky," I said, "that's grotesque."

"That's Knoxville," she said.

"So while they're arguing over who gets the body, word gets around the family can't pay the bill. Both of them start backpedaling. Neither wants him now—no money, no burial. So they do what any respectable undertakers would do." She smirked. "They leave him right there in the booth."

She flicked ash over the Tennessee marble balustrade.

"The bartender finally looks over and says, 'Somebody's gotta settle that tab.' The two drivers point at the corpse. Swear on it. Bartender's so mad he pulls out a revolver and shoots the dead man again."

She waited.

"Twice dead?" I said.

"Twice," she said, satisfied. "Slumped over a pickled-egg jar like he was praying for mercy."

"Becky, that didn't happen."

"Course it did," she said. "Right there on Depot, just east of Central. Ask anybody who was drinking back then—if they're still breathing."

She leaned back in the rocker.

"That's the problem with your generation," she said. "You keep looking for proof instead of listening for truth. I saw the way people lived. I saw the way they died. I loved every misfit in between."

"I know you did," I said.

She stubbed out her cigarette in a saucer and looked across my yard.

"If I go before you," she said, "promise me something."

"What's that?"

"Don't let them drag me into no beer joint. Unless it's to buy a round."

We sat a while, the afternoon light turning the porch gold.

I squinted at her. "You didn't just come to tell me a story, Beck B. What else is going on?"

She exhaled slowly, watching the smoke twist into the humid air.

"Just wanted to say thank you for your little poetry slam," she said. "The one where you left 'em speechless."

I groaned. "My slam, or yours?"

"Correct," she laughed. "All that posturing. All that solemn nodding. Like they were deciding the fate of Rome instead of whether somebody could walk their kids home safe from school."

She shook her head, bemused. "They think power lives in the room," she said. "In the microphones. In their own voices."

She tapped ash into the saucer.

"Power's already left by the time the meeting starts. All that's left is performance."

"And the rest of us?"

"We're the audience," she said. "Unless we bring a better story."

She smiled then—not sweet, not mean. Practical.

"That's why I tell you these things," she said. "Nobody remembers their speeches. But they remember a dead man shot twice because nobody wanted to pay for him."

I leaned back in my chair. "You ever get tired of it?"

"No," she said. "I just got clearer."

We spent the next two hours mapping her plan—zoning codes, favors owed, which reporters still took her calls. Becky could bend bureaucracy into theater, and she made me part of the act.

When she stood to leave, she tapped her watch and said she had "three more fires to start before dark." Then she was gone, gravel spitting, the truck's engine fading downhill.

• • •

The porch went quiet. Cicadas. Heat. Memory.

Her smoke still hung in the air—Marlboro Lights, hairspray, trouble. I let it linger.

Becky's kind didn't belong to any one story. She was Knoxville's unofficial memory keeper—half journalist, half provocateur, full-time witness. She knew where the bodies were buried because she'd registered most of their cousins to vote.

That story about the dead man on Depot—maybe it never happened. Not exactly like she told it. But it could have. And in this town, that matters.

When you're from East Tennessee, you learn that truth isn't a headline. It's what survives each retelling.

I shut the laptop and rocked a while in the chair, thinking about how she'd put it—proof versus truth.

Proof fades. Truth lingers.

Somewhere down on Depot, in old brick and beer-stained floors, the story's still there—grateful that someone like Becky was stubborn enough to keep it alive.

## Six

# THE MADAM AND THE TRASH CAN

This story is one of Becky Brewer's finest, and it's one I've tried to learn by heart. Hazel Davidson's place on Hoitt Avenue looked innocent enough if you didn't know any better. White clapboard, porch swing, window boxes filled with petunias that wilted the minute they touched the air around her. The sign by the porch still read Room for Rent, though no one had paid for a night's sleep there in years.

Hazel stood tall, her dark, glossy hair framing a face sharpened by years of style and survival. Her eyes missed nothing. Her perfume drifted through the air. When she greeted guests, you sensed the calculation beneath the laugh—a woman in control of the room.

She dressed in tailored skirts and sleeveless blouses for Sunday gatherings: nothing ostentatious, but everything coordinated—shoes, earrings, handbag. A poodle with a perfect cut and baby-blue nails accompanied her.

Inside, Hazel was staging her own kind of Sunday service. Fried chicken on silver trays. Pimento cheese in cut-glass bowls. A decanter of Early Times sweating beside a stack of hymnals no one had opened since the Eisenhower administration. The girls—Hazel never let anyone call them that—floated between the kitchen and parlor in sleeveless dresses and bright lipstick, carrying ashtrays.

Becky French Brewer had been there enough Sundays to know the rhythm: two hours of laughter, one hour of confession.

Hazel liked to play mother and priestess both, and if you stuck around till dusk, she might tell you who was sleeping with whom, or where a certain body was buried. She said it like gospel, and nobody doubted her.

That was why Becky went—what she called R&I: research and intelligence. Every political campaign in Knoxville and Knox County ran on gossip before it ran on votes, and Hazel's parlor was where most of the truth got edited.

You could pick up more intel there over a plate of fried chicken and collard greens spread out across Hazel's porcelain kitchen drainboard than you'd get in three weeks at the courthouse. Who was buying off whom, who was running out of cash, who'd been seen leaving the wrong house or the wrong bar after dark. Hazel had a way of making it sound like weather.

She didn't trade secrets for money. She traded them for attention, and she knew Becky was a woman who could be trusted.

Becky took notes in her head. The names, the slip-ups, the laughter too sharp to be innocent. She wasn't there to judge—she was there to remember.

If you worked in politics long enough in Knoxville, you learned that righteousness was mostly a matter of timing. And Hazel Davidson had the best timing in town.

That afternoon, the guest list leaned heavy on politics and perfume. A city councilman nursing a hangover. Two realtors who treated adultery like sport. And in the corner chair, Charles "Chubby" Smith himself—publisher of The Knoxville Journal, Knoxville's self-appointed Republican conscience.

Chubby was a large man, not just in body but in appetite. His laugh filled the room before he did. He could make any sentence sound like a headline.

"Hazel, darling," he said, forking a deviled egg, "you could run the Chamber of Commerce if you wanted. You've already got better attendance."

Hazel smiled and poured him another drink.

"Sugar, I don't recruit members. They recruit themselves."

He winked, satisfied, then turned. "Becky, you oughta come down to the newsroom sometime. See what an honest operation looks like."

Becky laughed, because that's what you do when you're dating the publisher and most of your friends live in moral gray.

He'd taken Becky to dinner twice that month—always at the Tropicana Room, the dim-lit basement bar off Gay Street next to the Andrew Johnson Hotel where late-night jazz covered up a multitude of sins. Always after his wife's charity meetings. She liked him in the way a girl likes a thunderstorm: powerful, noisy, dangerous up close.

Hazel caught her watching him and said, "Don't get lost in that one, baby. He writes his own absolution every morning."

Outside, cicadas rattled. Inside, the record player hissed through a Buddy Holly tune, and Hazel's poodle barked at the sound of a car door slamming somewhere down the block.

Then came the low hum of engines.

Hazel froze, hand mid-air with the cigarette. Chubby looked up, eyes narrowing behind his horn-rimmed glasses. Becky had heard that sound before—unmarked cars rolling slow, one after another. The Knoxville Morals Squad, making its rounds.

Hazel stubbed out her cigarette and exhaled.

"Well," she said, smoothing her dress, "looks like the Lord's decided to send visitors."

The girls scattered. One dove behind the piano, another straight through the kitchen and out the back door. Chubby stood but couldn't quite decide where to go. The big man who ran the city's news machine suddenly looked like a child caught in his daddy's liquor cabinet. Becky, nonplussed, remained poised and grinning on a kitchen stool next to the platter of fried chicken, cigarette in hand.

Hazel pointed toward the back porch. "Trash cans are empty. Pick one."

Chubby blinked, sweating, as if he thought she was joking.

She wasn't.

Becky watched him lumber down the steps, red-faced, cursing under his breath. The lid clanged shut, and the only sound left was the crickets.

Hazel turned, perfectly composed.

"You see, Becky? That's Knoxville for you. All our headlines end up in the garbage sooner or later."

Then she smiled and went to answer the knock at the front door.

Hazel opened the door before they could knock twice.

Detective Grady Moser stood there with two younger officers and a clipboard, hat in hand like a deacon about to apologize for something. His tie was crooked, his face too smooth for a man pretending to be righteous.

"Evening, Miz Davidson," he said, his voice half polite, half hungry. "We've had some complaints. Loud music, unfamiliar traffic. You mind if we take a look around?"

Hazel leaned against the doorframe, cigarette glowing.

"Well, Officer Moser, I do declare—if this is about my guests, I can assure you they're all God-fearing taxpayers. Some of 'em even work for the county."

She smiled.

He cleared his throat. "Just a routine inspection, ma'am."

Behind him, the younger cop shifted his weight, staring past her shoulder into the parlor. He looked too young to be in vice. Too curious to be innocent.

Hazel stepped aside. "Well, come on in, then. But wipe your feet. I just mopped."

From her chair near the window, Becky could see Moser's reflection in the mirror as he scanned the room—table still set, whiskey glasses half-full, chicken bones piled like evidence of a better hour.

Hazel followed his eyes and said, "You're welcome to a plate, honey. Lord knows the city don't pay you enough to ruin your own Sunday."

He didn't answer. Just moved toward the hallway, checking rooms that already knew too many secrets.

Outside, Chubby rustled in his metal coffin. Becky heard the faintest clang—lid shifting, maybe a muffled curse. A dog barked, sharp and accusing.

Hazel froze for a split second. Then, with perfect calm, she called out toward the back door.

"That's just a raccoon fiddling with my garbage, officer. I like to keep the garbage where I can see it."

Moser gave a small, suspicious smile. He knew she was mocking him, but the words didn't quite stick.

He opened the pantry, peeked into the kitchen, then came back to the parlor. "You running anything illegal here, Hazel?"

She laughed, soft and lazy. "Darlin', everything's illegal if you try hard enough."

That broke him. A small grin flickered and died. He reached into his coat and pulled out a folded paper—a search warrant that probably wouldn't hold up five minutes in court.

"Now, Hazel—" he began, but she cut him off, lifting her hand.

"Don't 'now Hazel' me, Grady. You know who signs your paycheck. Same folks eating my deviled eggs last week."

The room went still. Even the ceiling fan seemed to pause.

Then she reached for her purse, drew out a small envelope—brown, folded twice—and set it on the silver tray beside the whiskey.

"For the trouble," she said. "And the gas it took to get here."

He looked at it, then at her, and nodded—just a ghost of a nod.

He tucked the envelope into his jacket. "We'll file this under community relations."

"Good idea," Hazel said, lighting another cigarette. "And tell the chief I'll pray for him next Sunday—if I can remember which church he goes to."

They left without taking notes. The youngest one tipped his hat to Becky on the way out, eyes full of questions he'd never be old enough to ask.

When the sound of engines faded, Hazel waited a long minute before calling out, "You can come up for air now, Mr. Publisher."

The trash can lid clanged, then lifted, and Chubby emerged—sweating, pale, eyes wide like a child who's seen a ghost.

Hazel handed him a towel. "Honey, you smell like last week's paper under a mess of chitlins on Market Square," she said.

He tried to laugh, but the sound came out flat. "You could've warned me."

"I just did," she said. "Next time, bring your own headline."

Becky couldn't help it—she started laughing.

Hazel smiled, poured three bourbons, handed one to Chubby and one to Becky.

"To Knoxville," she said. "Where the garbage is cleaner than the people."

They drank to that.

• • •

Morning came gray and damp.

Becky bought a Knoxville Journal from the box outside Long's Drug Store, still damp with dew. Front page: VICE RAID CLEANS HOUSE—PROMINENT CITIZENS COOPERATE

No names. No addresses. No photographs. He knew better than to mess with Hazel Davidson.

Just the usual sermon about "moral integrity" and "the importance of vigilance." Chubby's own byline sat smugly at the top, like he'd written it from some lofty, god-fearing perch—not from inside a trash can full of chicken bones and bourbon bottles.

Becky read it twice, standing there on the sidewalk, looking for signs. She felt something cold settle behind her ribs. Not anger, not shock—just realization that every city lies about itself, and every lie needs someone to write it down.

By afternoon, Hazel's house looked as if nothing had happened. Laundry on the line. Radio humming gospel. The air already forgiving.

Becky slipped an envelope into her mailbox—a clipping of the article, folded once, with a note scribbled on the back in blue ink:

"Guess you can't make clean soap without some kinda lie.—B."

Hazel called that evening.

"Well, baby, you've got to admire him," she said. "Takes a real newspaperman to hide inside his own story."

Becky could hear the clink of her ice glass, the slow exhale of smoke.

"They'll come back," Hazel said. "They always do. Knoxville men are like stray dogs—bark all night, then come scratchin' at your door."

She wasn't wrong.

A few weeks later, Chubby invited Becky to dinner again, all smiles and apologies. She told him she was busy washing her hair. He laughed, thinking it was a joke.

Hazel kept her Sunday gatherings smaller after that. Fewer men in suits, more women who didn't flinch when the sirens passed. She liked to say she was redecorating.

Sometimes, when the air got too still, Becky would think about that night—the flash of police lights on Hazel's white porch, the sound of

Chubby's breath echoing inside that metal drum, and Hazel, standing there in her pearls, playing Knoxville's oldest game: sin and survival.

• • •

Years later, Becky told me the story again—three times, maybe four—each retelling slower, as if she wanted to be sure I'd get it right. We were in a bar off Central Avenue, her drinking sweet tea and me two bourbons deep, the jukebox low and mournful. Someone at the counter asked if it really happened.

I smiled, stirred my drink, and said, "True enough for Knoxville. The publisher of the Journal hid in a garbage can while his paper shouted about sin. The only clean thing that night was the whiskey."

They laughed. I didn't. Becky just watched me over her glass, the corners of her mouth curling into something between pride and pity. She'd been waiting for that moment—when I finally understood that in Knoxville, truth doesn't need proof, only timing.

• • •

Hazel Davidson was a real Knoxville figure—born in 1923 near Strawberry Plains, once a model, later known as the "playgirl" who ran a discreet network of brothels from the 2300 block of Hoitt Avenue and Riverside Drive. Her name appears in court records and local archives through the 1960s and '70s, often linked to vice raids that produced more headlines than convictions.

Charles "Chubby" Smith died in 1980 when his World War II fighter plane crashed on a northeast Georgia farm.

The tale of the *Madam and the Trash Can* comes from Knoxville's oral tradition, passed down by the late Becky French Brewer, who swore the publisher of *The Knoxville Journal* once hid in Hazel's trash can during a vice raid. Whether fact or fiction, it remains one of the city's favorite parables about sin, survival, and public virtue gone private.

Seven

# LYNCH MOB ON THE GAY STREET BRIDGE

Friday was often the day Becky liked to disappear into East Knoxville. We'd dropped off a stack of Park City books at barber shops, restaurants, and local stores, places kept running by people who showed up every day and didn't need to explain themselves. These were our people, and each promised to put them where people could see them, which meant near the cash register and nowhere near the sports magazines. That was good enough for us.

From there, we walked over to The Lunch House, where nothing on the menu pretended to be new and the plates arrived already knowing what you'd ordered. Meat and three. Country ham for Becky, meatloaf for me, green beans and carrots cooked long past apology, mashed potatoes holding their shape because that was their job. Sweet tea in Styrofoam cups so thin you could feel the cold through them. Becky said that was how you knew a place wasn't lying to you.

We ate slowly. Becky read the room, clocking who belonged, who was visiting, who had something to say but wouldn't. Not faces—positions. A state senator. A newspaper reporter. Two county commissioners sitting with a couple of preachers. Power didn't announce itself; it clustered.

When we finished, Becky crushed the lid down on her tea cup, stood, and said, "You driving or am I?"

Her pickup back at home, we took her Cadillac Fleetwood, the size of a small municipal building, hunter green paint holding on by habit rather than polish. The bench seat swallowed us whole. Becky drove with one hand, elbow out the window, the other already fishing for a cigarette she wouldn't light until we were parked.

We headed toward Chilhowee Park, past what used to be ambition and now only remembered itself. Becky pulled up near the old marble bandstand, the last surviving piece of the 1910 Appalachian Exposition, still standing there without explanation or apology. Marble columns stained with time, not neglect. There's a difference.

We took our tea and sat under the bandstand, the afternoon stretched wide and patient. I waited until Becky settled in, crossed her legs, and lit the cigarette.

"Alright," she said. "What've you got?"

I pulled out the photocopies. "Becky," I said, "I know how much you like your hookers and murders. You're gonna love this one."

She laughed once, sharp. "Careful," she said. "That's a limited audience."

"This starts with a deathbed confession," I said. "1896. Woman named Lizzie Hickman. Described in the paper as a 'notorious prostitute,' which is how you know they thought the label took care of all of it."

Becky leaned back against the marble, eyes narrowing. "Go on."

"She says the wrong man was lynched. Says she's known it for years. Says that Lee Sellers didn't do it, and the real killer walked free."

That got her full attention. "Knoxville?" she asked.

"Knoxville," I said. "September 1885. Traveling salesman named Edward Maines gets murdered and robbed. Not far from here. Over off Riverside Drive, I think."

Edward Maines was a traveling salesman from Athens, Tennessee, moving through East Knoxville on business in early September of 1885. He represented the C.M. McClung Company, one of Knoxville's rising mercantile houses, and like many salesmen of the period, he carried his earnings in cash—collections made face to face, commissions folded into risk. The papers never lingered on his biography beyond that, but they emphasized what mattered: he was known to have money on him, and he was far enough from home to be vulnerable.

That night, Maines had been drinking, moving through saloons and brothels along Central Avenue. When his body was found, he had been shot in the back of the head and robbed. Newspapers put the amount taken at anywhere between one and fifteen hundred dollars—enough money to turn suspicion into urgency before evidence ever had a chance to settle.

"Town arrests two men," I said. "One of them never sees a courtroom. One of them does."

The second man was Ike Wright. Unlike Sellers, Wright was not dragged from a cell or paraded through the streets. He remained available to the courts, which meant the town could afford to be patient with him. The newspapers treated the case as already resolved. Maines's profession, his cash, and his hometown were foregrounded; Sellers's guilt was assumed. Reports stressed speed—swift arrest, swift certainty—as if delay itself were dangerous. Justice was framed as something that needed to happen before questions could interfere.

Wright's case moved slowly enough to feel civilized. Sellers's did not. That difference had nothing to do with evidence and everything to do with timing, temperament, and who a crowd decides is safe to wait on.

Lee Sellers, age 22, was arrested quickly. White. Born in Tennessee. What little the papers say about him places him on the margins—no prominent family, no standing worth protecting, no biography the town felt obliged to preserve. He was accused before he was understood, and understood only through accusation.

"A mob that included men from Athens and Knoxville stormed the jail," I said. "And this was not a crowd that rushed. It marched."

The papers were careful about that. They wanted it understood that Knoxville did this neatly—keys surrendered, men masked but composed, pistols fired more out of ritual than rage. Some came from Athens. Others joined along the way. A few stepped out of a dance still dressed for it.

"Middle of the night."

The jail keys were surrendered, but the cell door was smashed anyway. Sellers resisted. He wounded one of the men trying to restrain him, and that resistance was treated not as desperation but as proof that restraint had been a mistake.

"Marched him down Gay Street," I said. "Took him to the bridge."

Becky exhaled slowly. "Name again?" she said.

"Lee Sellers."

She shook her head once. "Don't know it."

"Exactly," I said. "Neither did I."

They dragged him down Gay Street to the bridge. A rope was thrown over a beam. The hanging failed. Sellers climbed the rope, alive and struggling. The crowd opened fire. Men ran for ladders to finish what the rope had not.

That detail stayed with me. The papers didn't quite know where to put it. A man trying to live complicates a story that's already been agreed upon.

I told her about the mob. About the rope. About the shots fired when the hanging didn't go fast enough. About how the papers said he pleaded innocence, and then begged the mob to kill him quickly.

Whether he fell or was thrown, Sellers went over the side into the Tennessee River below, already shot. The river did not offer escape. It carried his body downstream, where it was recovered and identified as the town's answer.

With Sellers dead, Wright's prosecution cooled. The urgency evaporated. What had demanded immediate resolution the night before now required deliberation, and deliberation, in Knoxville then as now, was a reliable way to let things dissolve.

"And then, Becky," I said, "eleven years later, Lizzie Hickman decides she's done carrying it."

Becky tapped ash into the grass. "Who'd she say did it?"

"Ike Wright," I said. "And she wasn't the only one. Another man said the same thing before he died. People heard it. People remembered it."

"And?" Becky said.

"And nothing," I said. "No retrial. No apology. Just a paragraph buried in the paper like an afterthought."

Lizzie Hickman was described by the papers as a prostitute and known associate of the men involved—a label that made her confession easier to dismiss once it became inconvenient. Dying in 1896, she named Ike Wright as the real killer—a name she had known long before the mob ever learned Sellers's—and said Lee Sellers had been innocent.

The same paper that couldn't wait for Sellers had all the time in the world for Lizzie Hickman. Eleven years was apparently the right distance for truth—far enough away not to require action. Another man, Sam Doggett, had said the same before his own death. Their words arrived only after the town no longer had to act on them.

Becky stared out across the park, past the bandstand, past the paths where kids rode bikes now without knowing what used to be paraded through here.

"So the town picked wrong," she said.

"This town picks its winners and losers awfully fast, Becky," I said.

She nodded. "That's the worst part, isn't it?"

We sat there a moment, the Fleetwood ticking quietly behind us, the marble cool under our backs, silence that doesn't argue back.

"Alright," Becky said, closing her eyes in the afternoon sun. "Start again, from the beginning. I want to hear the whole thing again."

And I did, knowing she would pick every detail apart without mercy.

And she did.

Critically, Lee Sellers and Lizzie Hickman survive only where the moment caught them—newsprint and a death register. No later histories take them up. No civic memory carries them forward. What remains is not a record so much as a set of edges: names, dates, accusations, and a silence that follows.

The lynching on the Gay Street Bridge was moral theater—a way to metabolize fear, crime, and social instability in a rapidly urbanizing Appalachian city.

It was reported nationally, including in the New York Times and the Chicago Tribune.

Sellers's case shaped later legal behavior, including the speed and theatricality of the Hicks Carmichael trial in 1888. Lee Sellers was white, obscure, and unprotected—his name carried nationally only because of how publicly the town chose to erase him. Even now, he survives mostly as a citation, not a memory.

That's how stories like this disappear. Not all at once, but by being left where the archive stops looking. Becky didn't listen to be moved. She listened to make sure the truth could survive being said aloud.

## Eight
# WHAT THIS TOWN COULD TOLERATE

Becky carried the thick manila folder the same way she brought most things to my porch—tucked under her arm like it might still bite if handled wrong. She treated information the way other people treated animals: cautiously, with respect for teeth.

"If you cut your arm off at the elbow, Doug, I'll cut mine off at the shoulder," Becky grinned. "I'll see your Lee Sellers case and raise you one Maude Moore."

It was a late summer afternoon, and I was working from home on the front porch. Bright sunlight streamed over Greystone Mansion hard enough that I was working in sunglasses.

Becky didn't sit right away. She stood there flipping pages, squinting at me, then at the photocopy of old newsprint like it had personally offended her.

"You look pretty stupid working on the computer with those sunglasses on."

I smiled, ignoring the dig.

"What can I do for ya, Beck B?"

"Now this one," she said, tapping the paper, "this town never did know what to do with Maude—just like Evelyn Hazen."

Becky liked cases that resisted conclusion. She mistrusted anything that ended neatly, especially when the town seemed relieved it had. And she paid attention to women the way archivists pay attention to missing pages. Not because they were rare, but because their absence and removal were often patterned. In

Knoxville, women didn't vanish from the record by accident. They were edited out once they'd served the story.

The file was thin in the way old crimes usually are. One page from the *Atlanta Semi-Weekly Journal*, 1919. A photograph of a woman everyone insisted on calling pretty before they called her anything else. Maude Moore. Charged with killing a Knoxville businessman named LeRoy Harth. Wealthy. Well known. Diamond ring worth more than a poor man's farm, according to her lawyer, who knew exactly what he was doing when he said it.

Becky sat, my grandmother's 90-year old metal rocker creaking and bouncing. She handed me the paper.

"Read it out loud," she said. "Go full Perry Mason."

So I did. *Maude Moore fainted as she left the stand*, I began.

That was the first line that mattered. Everything after was just people arguing over who deserved to fall.

According to the paper, Maude said she shot Harth in self-defense. Defense of her honor. Defense of her life.

The prosecution tried to make it about robbery, about planning, about a man named Martin Hunter and a note to Maude that sounded guilty because it didn't sound like anything at all.

*Tear those letters up. I am gone. Please keep quiet.*

Becky snorted. "That's not a criminal mastermind," she said. "That's a man who panicked halfway through his own bad idea."

The courtroom, according to the paper, was packed. Not just full—invested. People hissed at witnesses they didn't like. Applauded the defense like it was a tent revival. Someone started collecting money for Maude's legal fund. Chattanooga women, the article said, as if that explained everything.

Courtrooms like that weren't about truth. They were about rehearsal—teaching a town how to feel afterward. Verdicts mattered less than the lesson everyone agreed to carry home.

The lawyer didn't argue innocence. He argued righteousness. Said Maude ought to have a cross pinned on her for killing Harth. Said she probably saved other women from being debauched. The paper printed that word like it weighed a hundred pounds.

Becky leaned back, eyes closed, rocking slightly.

"You hear that?" she said.

"Hear what?"

"The town deciding what kind of story it wanted."

Harth, in this version, became a type instead of a man. Money. Whiskey. Automobile. Lust. The paper practically undressed him in public. Even admitted—almost casually—that he was on a mission of immorality. As if that settled it. As if motive could substitute for sequence.

Maude, meanwhile, never got more specific than fainted, pretty, defendant. No interior life allowed. Just a body reacting to pressure. Specific women are hard to control. Types are easy. Once Maude became a symbol—honor, temptation, hysteria—the town could stop worrying about what she might actually say.

Becky lit a cigarette without asking, which was how I knew she was settling in. She smoked like she was still arguing with people who weren't present, drawing hard, exhaling sideways, as if the room itself were wrong.

"Nobody in that room cared," she said, "what actually happened once they realized they could use it."

She flicked ash into an empty mason jar that had once held honey, then screws, then nothing at all.

The paper never says where Maude learned to shoot. It never says whether Harth touched her first, or how close he was standing, or whether the gun surprised either of them when it went off. It doesn't even settle who fired—whether it was Maude herself, or another man entirely: Martin Hunter.

Instead, it gives us fainting, diamonds, applause, and the satisfying hiss of a crowd disciplining the wrong witness.

That's not reportage. That's moral choreography.

Becky leaned forward. "This town loves a woman who knows her place," she said, "and hates her even more when she steps out of it."

In the Maude Moore version, the reasons were tidy. Honor. Life. A rich man with appetites and a ring fat enough to become metaphor. The story reduced itself efficiently.

The prosecution wanted motive you could diagram. Hunter was charged as an accomplice, accused of helping arrange the meeting, handling money afterward, and fleeing with Maude once Harth was dead.

But the town wasn't buying any complicated stories of love or betrayal.

Knoxville wanted release. Relief is easier to organize than truth, and far easier to live with afterward.

"You ever notice," Becky said, "how fainting shows up right when a woman's done being useful?"

Maude fainted after she testified. After she gave them the part they needed. They characterized her as the right kind of fragile. The tragic *Knoxville Girl* archetype. Collapse as punctuation. The body closing the argument when language ran out.

I told her the dying declaration bothered me, the way Harth supposedly said she shot him and guessed she meant to rob him, the word "guessed" doing all the work for a man who didn't live long enough to clarify.

"A guess," Becky said, "is what you offer when you don't want to be responsible for the ending."

She thought the dying man gave them exactly enough ambiguity to work with. Enough to fuel both sides. Enough to keep the case alive without ever letting it resolve.

That's how stories survive a century: not by accuracy, but by refusing to settle.

What the paper also didn't offer was an ending.

Within a year, Maude Moore and Martin Hunter would both step out of Knoxville's reach, leaving behind letters, rumors, and just enough direction to make pursuit expensive and certainty impossible.

She knocked ash into the jar again and said another name, casually, as if it had been waiting its turn. "Now compare that to Evelyn Hazen."

Knoxville could forgive a woman who disappeared. What it couldn't tolerate was one who stayed and asked to be believed. She didn't need to explain who Evelyn Hazen was. Knoxville has been explaining her for decades.

Evelyn sued the man who promised to marry her and didn't. Carried the case up through Kentucky courts in the 1930s. Won a judgment so large the papers couldn't resist printing the number like a dare. Proof, on paper, that the law could still punish a certain kind of male cruelty.

"And yet," Becky said, "she paid for it anyway."

Because winning didn't end Evelyn Hazen's story. It cracked it open. She had to testify to intimacy, justify believing, justify waiting, justify why a woman would organize her life around a promise that had never been meant to be kept.

She won the case, lost her job, lost her standing, and never truly collected the prize that made her famous. The law gave Evelyn a number and called it justice. The town answered with consequences the courts didn't track. Respectability, once revoked, doesn't come back with interest.

Knoxville remembered her, all right—but mostly as a cautionary tale, not a person. She was preserved the way towns preserve lessons: stripped of context, polished for reuse, and emptied of anything that might complicate the warning.

Evelyn still owned the antebellum family home, the Mabry-Hazen House on Mabry's Hill just east of downtown. Prime real estate was another reason Evelyn was never forgotten, even if she was mocked for years by the blue bloods of Knoxville.

"In being forgotten," Becky said, "it sounds like Maude may have gotten the better deal."

Maude didn't sue. She didn't wait fifteen years for the law to validate her patience. She acted in a moment that couldn't be civilized into precedent. Her case didn't offer society a way to feel enlightened afterward. It offered applause in the room and discomfort once the door closed.

Evelyn Hazen fit a shape the courts and papers could reuse.

Maude Moore didn't. Maude ended her story too honestly, too violently, too close to the raw exchange nobody wanted preserved.

Becky lit another cigarette.

"One woman got a judgment," she said. "The other got silence."

And silence, around here, has always been the heavier sentence.

"So where do you think they went?"

Becky didn't answer right away. She took a drag, watched the smoke thin out over the porch rail, and smiled the way she did when a question earned itself.

"Not where people like to imagine," she said. "Not running hand in hand toward romance or reinvention. That's a story for people who've never had to disappear."

An escape to Italy was mentioned in one of the letters. That Martin supposedly claimed he was sailing. That it sounded theatrical enough to be either true or a lie meant to waste time.

"Exactly," Becky said. "You don't tell the truth when you're trying to leave. You tell something interesting."

She thought they went somewhere dull. Somewhere anonymity did the heavy lifting. A mill town that didn't ask questions. A river city where names were interchangeable. A place where a woman with a steady hand and a man who knew when to keep quiet could pass without explanation.

"People forget," she said, "how easy it was to vanish if you stopped insisting on being someone."

I asked if she thought they stayed together.

"Long enough," she shrugged. "That's usually the answer."

She said maybe they split once the danger thinned out. Maybe they didn't. Maybe the point wasn't love or loyalty but shared timing—two people who knew the moment had passed and refused to hang around for the moral of the story.

"They didn't want absolution," she said. "They wanted distance."

I said it sounded lonely.

She nodded. "Running always is," she said. "But so is staying when the town's already decided what you're for."

Becky ground out her cigarette and stood, brushing ash from her jeans.

"They didn't become legends," she said. "They became unremarkable."

Becky gave me a half-smile, like she wasn't entirely sure whether that was tragedy or mercy.

Knoxville remembers men by what they controlled. It remembers women by how neatly they exit the frame.

"And that," she said, "might've been the bravest thing either of them ever did."

## Nine
# KINGPIN

Becky neglected to tell me who was coming to dinner. She said she had an old friend she wanted me to meet. Someone she'd known a long time. Someone who had stories that were beginning to slip their moorings, not because he was unreliable, but because time was beginning to reorder how he was remembered. She said she wanted my help writing his story down before that happened.

That was all.

We planned it the way Southerners plan things that matter without admitting they matter. Steak. A big ol' iceberg lettuce wedge with thousand island dressing like they used to serve at the Regas Restaurant. A decent bottle of bourbon. Candles on the porch because the light inside felt like it would ask questions. I assumed we were doing what we'd done a hundred times before—letting the evening wander until it found something honest.

When Don Walker arrived, he did not arrive like a man whose name once anchored federal indictments.

He arrived like a neighbor.

He remembered my street, my house, and the former owner, bluegrass legend Curly Dan Bailey, who was Cas Walker's old radio announcer.

Don was already in his seventies then, smaller than I expected, dressed plainly, carrying himself with the careful economy of someone who had learned early when movement attracted attention and when it did not. He shook my hand with a grip that lingered just long enough to register, then loosened, measured, deliberate.

If I knew who he was that night, I didn't know it consciously. I knew only that Becky watched him with a particular attentiveness she reserved for people who had lived inside systems rather than merely alongside them. I knew she poured his drink herself. I knew she steered the conversation gently, letting it circle without landing, giving him space to decide how much he intended to reveal.

Don grew up poorer than dirt. One of nearly a dozen children. A mother who worked the knitting mills. Shoes that came late, if they came at all. Hunger that wasn't dramatic enough to make stories out of, but persistent enough to teach lessons early. He learned how informal economies replaced formal ones long before he learned the language people later used to excuse them.

By the time Knoxville knew his name, he had already learned how cities functioned.

We talked about small things at first. The way neighborhoods had changed. The way certain roads still carried memory even after the businesses along them disappeared. He talked about clubs he'd run in his younger years, but not with pride or apology. Just fact. Clubs all over town. Clubs across the Southeast. Places that opened and closed depending on who needed them open and who needed them quiet.

He had always been generous with kids in the neighborhood. That part came up naturally, without emphasis. He said it the way men say things they don't consider remarkable. If a widow needed a tree cut down, it got cut. If a family needed groceries, someone made sure they appeared. Charity, for him, was not a performance. It was a kind of bookkeeping.

At some point Becky shifted the conversation without announcing it. She didn't ask for gossip. She didn't ask him to incriminate himself or anyone else. She wanted to talk about how Knoxville had always been "wide open," her euphemism for the structure of roadside casinos and clubs. She asked him to help us place Knoxville's civic respectability beside the machinery that produced it, without letting either pretend the other didn't exist.

She was explicit about what she wanted and what she didn't. Names where the public record already existed. Description where it didn't. Sequence over spectacle. She wanted a story that could survive daylight.

Don listened. He hadn't made up his mind yet.

He turned his glass slightly, aligning the rim with the edge of the table, a small act of calibration.

Becky asked him where it began.

She didn't ask about charges or courtrooms. She asked when Knoxville first made sense to him.

Don smiled at that, brief and unguarded.

"You want the honest answer?" he said.

"That's usually what I'm after," Becky said.

He took a moment, looking past her, toward the street, as if confirming the world was still arranged the way he remembered it.

"It started with rooms," he said. "Places people went when they wanted to feel normal doing things they didn't want discussed."

Becky didn't interrupt. She let him roll, which was unusual for her.

"The Southland. The C'est Bon. The Senators Club. Pick a name. Folks remember the names because they sound colorful now. Back then they sounded practical. Supper club. Athletic club. Country club. Those weren't aspirations. They were shields."

She asked what they shielded.

"Everyone," he said. "Owners. Customers. The city itself. Once a place wore the right label, people relaxed. Inspectors relaxed. Ministers relaxed. The paper relaxed. Things could move without anyone having to explain themselves."

"What things?" Becky asked.

Don shrugged.

"Money, mostly. Favors. Introductions. Promises that didn't need to be written down. You'd be surprised how little has to be said once everyone agrees to the same silence."

Becky asked whether he thought of it as organized crime.

He shook his head, amused.

"That makes it sound louder than it was," he said. "What held it together wasn't fear. It was familiarity. Everybody knew who they were dealing with. Everybody knew what would happen if they embarrassed the wrong person. Violence happened, sure, but it wasn't how things ran. Things ran on understanding."

She asked how far that understanding traveled.

"Further than the city limits," he said. "Roadside casinos. Clubs that survived because nobody respectable wanted to claim them. Highways mattered more than neighborhoods. If you controlled how people and money moved between places, you didn't have to own much outright."

Becky said expansion changes the temperature.

"It does," Don said. "More money brings more interest. Interest brings pressure."

"From where?" she asked.

He glanced toward the street, then back to Becky.

"From both sides," he said. "The law starts paying closer attention. So do people who already think the territory belongs to them."

Becky nodded.

"That's usually where the trouble starts," she said.

Don smiled again, thinner this time.

"That's what got me, honey," he said. "I got careless."

The U.S. Marshals began staking out one of his Knoxville bars. Around the same time, men connected to New Orleans interests started showing up uninvited, mistaking proximity for permission. Those pressures collided one night in a way no one planned.

Becky asked him when it stopped feeling manageable.

Don didn't answer right away. He took a sip, then another, buying time.

"Long before I admitted it," he said. "That's usually how it goes."

She didn't press. She never did. She let the silence do the work.

"I was making money the old way at first," he said. "Cash. Clubs. Side rooms. Things that stayed inside the building. Things I could see."

Becky said, "And then?"

"And then the eighties showed up," he said. "Different scale. Different speed. Cocaine."

He shook his head again.

"Cocaine didn't care about Knoxville," he said. "It just passed through it."

Becky leaned forward a little.

"They moved it through the clubs."

He nodded.

"Because when you already control the rooms," he said, "staff, schedules, deliveries—nobody questioned anything that already belonged."

He talked about it the way men do when they've replayed the logic too many times to count.

"For places like Knoxville, it always starts small," he said. "Then it wasn't. Kilos don't hide the way envelopes do. They make you sloppy. They make you believe your own infrastructure."

Becky asked whether he knew he was pushing it.

"I knew," he said. "I just thought I knew better."

That was where the greed crept in—not loud, not desperate, just confident. He had survived worse things than attention. He had paid people before. He had smoothed problems over with money, favors, introductions.

"You think that the clubs insulate you," he said. "That the names on the doors still meant something."

They didn't anymore.

"The Marshals started watching one of my Knoxville places," he said. "I noticed, but I didn't change enough."

Becky asked why.

"Because business was moving," he said. "And when business is moving, you convince yourself you can outrun the consequences."

He said the New Orleans people arrived around the same time. Not invited. Not subtle.

"They saw volume," he said. "They saw routes. They thought that meant ownership."

Becky said, "And that doesn't end well."

"No," he said. "It never does."

The night he got shot in Fountain City came out of overlapping assumptions. People watching who shouldn't have been there. People enforcing things they hadn't earned. Nobody coordinating. Nobody backing off.

He didn't dramatize it.

"I walked outside," he said. "Next thing I knew, I was on the ground."

He lived. That part still surprised him.

The rest moved fast. Federal charges. Statutes written for examples, not exceptions. Paperwork that reduced a decade of complexity to a single phrase.

He became the first person in East Tennessee arrested and convicted under the new drug kingpin statute. I'd learn the details later, but at the time I just sat there and kept my mouth shut.

Becky didn't recount the history. She didn't need to. We could both see it in his eyes.

"That's when I understood," Don said. "Not that I was done. That the structure didn't care whether I was there anymore."

He looked at her then, not defensive, not proud.

"I wasn't some mastermind," he said. "I was a man who pushed his luck after it stopped being luck."

The porch went quiet again. Somewhere down the block a car passed, slow, unimportant.

Becky closed her notebook, not because the story was finished, but because this part finally was.

After his conviction and nine years in federal prison, Don got out. As a convicted felon, however, he could not legally operate businesses. That did not mean the businesses disappeared. It meant they were handed over to other people to run how they saw fit.

What struck me, listening, was how little emphasis he placed on the kingpin statute itself. Civility and violence were not opposites in Knoxville. They were paired tools. Charity did not negate harm. It organized it.

Later in the evening, we were all pretty relaxed. Becky didn't drink, but she was rolling a joint as our conversation drifted toward the Butchers, not as gossip, but as context.

Everyone in Knoxville knew the name. Jake and C.H. Butcher had built United American Bank into a regional empire during the 1970s and early 1980s, financing development, the 1982 World's Fair, underwriting civic ambition, and placing themselves at the center of the city's idea of progress. The collapse came fast. Federal investigations exposed reckless lending, insider deals, and political pressure applied as standard operating procedure. When the bank failed in 1983, it wiped out depositors, embarrassed regulators, and left Knoxville with a skyline built on bad paper.

Jake Butcher built the Whirlwind estate in Anderson County in the 1970s. It sat above the river on land acquired long before the bank, secluded, old, and difficult to access.

With Don across the table, Becky asked if he'd ever heard about a drug tunnel that ran from the house to the river.

Don said he'd heard the same rumors everyone else had.

It was the kind of detail that people liked to believe because it made the system feel engineered rather than improvised. Don dismissed it out of hand.

No one at the table tried to connect those facts into a theory. Knoxville had never needed tunnels to move power. It had banks, land, and a talent for letting certain stories end early.

By the time the candles burned down and the porch settled back into darkness, Becky had what she needed. Don declined the offer to let us write his story, and he did it without drama. He said it kindly, the way someone does when they know exactly what follows from saying yes.

A book like that, he said, wouldn't land cleanly. Too many people still carried pieces of it. Too many lives had been built adjacent to the wreckage. Letting it stay unfinished felt, to him, like a form of responsibility.

I respected that then. I understood it more later.

What Becky had been after wasn't permission. It was orientation. She wanted to know where to look, which rooms mattered, and which parts of Knoxville's history were doing the quiet work of holding everything else in place. Don gave her that much. He spoke in sequences, not defenses. He described how things moved, where they paused, and how order was maintained long before anyone started calling it criminal.

After that, the rest was research.

The public record filled in what conversation could not. Court filings. Old zoning maps. Liquor licenses. Charters for athletic clubs that never hosted athletics. Newsprint that learned how to say everything sideways. The story existed whether Don participated in it or not. It always had.

Only later did I understand who I had shared that porch with. Only later did the documents catch up to the man who had been careful with his words and precise with his silences.

Becky already knew where to begin, because in Knoxville the Southland and the C'est Bon always come first, teaching the city its habits in private rooms before those habits harden into a system.

• • •

The Southland sat out on Alcoa Highway, opened in the late 1930s, a supper club in the years when Knoxville was learning how to dress appetite up as leisure. Horseshoe neon. White tablecloths. A bandstand sized to look modest while doing serious work.

On paper, it was an athletic club. That designation mattered. It allowed membership rules to substitute for oversight and made certain questions inappropriate by default. Who belonged was less important than who did not, and why.

Inside, the music ran standards that never asked for attention—arrangements designed to smooth conversation rather than interrupt it. Men with lapel pins treated the room like neutral territory. Contractors talked zoning. Bankers talked little. Politics happened without naming itself.

Cash moved without ceremony.

What Don explained on the porch was that the Southland trained Knoxville in a particular reflex: how to let illegal activity exist comfortably inside legal language. Dice were never called dice. Bets were "after." Rooms behind rooms existed without signs. Ledgers recorded presence rather than purpose.

The Southland did not hide itself. It taught the city how to look past it.

• • •

By the late 1940s, Knoxville wanted something that looked more ambitious.

Around 1949, the C'est Bon Athletic & Country Club rose from the same foundation but aimed higher. Where the Southland had worn roadhouse manners, the C'est Bon adopted continental affectation. Cursive neon replaced block letters. Shrimp cocktail replaced catfish. Jazz arrived filtered through respectability.

The language remained the same. "Athletic." "Country." The paperwork still did its job.

What changed was confidence.

The clientele shifted upward—TVA engineers, bankers, state officials—men who preferred to believe culture itself conferred immunity. The bandstand doubled in size. The egos followed.

Don described the C'est Bon not as escalation, but as refinement. The machinery did not change. It learned better lighting.

• • •

When the C'est Bon burned, it burned fast.

A Saturday-night crowd. A ceiling dressed in palms. Wood and vinyl catching as soon as the air reached it. Fire ran toward the highway in a single, decisive push.

Officially, it was electrical. Unofficially, it was speculated as instruction. One door reported jammed. Shoes recovered from the ash, separated from their owners by nothing more than panic and timing.

The paper ran a filler: ELECTRICAL SHORT SUSPECTED AT C'EST BON FIRE.

What Don said on the porch was that fires rarely ended operations. They often cleared out old debts.

The rebuild came with a new name—the Senators Club—and the same machinery underneath. Wiring was replaced. Safes were relocated. Cash routes adjusted. The business continued.

• • •

Knoxville learned another lesson: destruction could be rehabilitative, provided it arrived with the right explanation.

What followed the clubs was not chaos. It was organization.

The lodges provided the necessary architecture. The Shriners, the Elks, the other Masonic Lodges—each offered something the clubs could not: daylight legitimacy. Their meeting halls created a civic overlay where gambling, favors, and money movement could exist under the language of fellowship and benevolence. The same men who sat in the back rooms at Southland and the C'est Bon now presided over raffles, poker nights, and charity events with printed programs and rotating committees.

The lodges allowed activity to pass between worlds without friction. A poker night raised money for children's hospitals. A roulette wheel funded scholarships. Bingo games underwrote church repairs. Every transaction was technically for a cause, which meant no one had to ask what else it accomplished.

This was where Knoxville perfected a particular moral posture: outcomes mattered more than methods, and generosity functioned as a kind of retroactive permission. If money ended up doing good, then its origin could remain politely unexamined.

The lodges didn't hide vice. They domesticated it. They were civic glue. I saw that up close. For a time, I was inside it—married into it. Our rehearsal dinner was held at Kerbela Shrine Temple. The Shriners, the Jesters, the Daughters of the Nile—rowdy, generous, tightly bonded. After that came the rhythm: countless fundraisers, casino nights, unofficial lotteries, games of chance that predated the state lottery by decades.

When a widow needed a tree cut down, men arrived. When a child needed school supplies, they appeared anonymously. When a community needed funding faster than official channels allowed, the money surfaced.

This was not random kindness. It was reputational infrastructure.

The genius of the system lay in its asymmetry. Gratitude accumulated downward, while accountability never traveled upward. People remembered who helped them. They did not ask how those helpers were protected.

What Knoxville learned, over decades, was that charity could absorb violence, illegality, and silence without losing its moral authority. Good works created a buffer that insulated entire networks from scrutiny. To challenge the system meant challenging the benefits it quietly distributed.

When the feds finally intervened—when new statutes made it possible to name kingpins rather than prosecute only their intermediaries—the shock was not moral. It was procedural.

Don Walker became the first person in East Tennessee arrested and convicted under the new federal drug kingpin statute. That fact mattered less for what it revealed than for what it disrupted. The statute collapsed the distance between charity and command. It forced the system to acknowledge hierarchy.

Even then, Knoxville responded with discipline rather than outrage.

Don served his time. He returned. He went back to church. He worked. He stayed visible but subdued. The city did not disown him. It reabsorbed him.

A later column by former U.S. Congressman John Duncan Jr. puts it all in perspective, not as sentiment but as evidence of the system.

• • •

In 2024, former Congressman John Duncan Jr.—long one of Knoxville's most durable political figures—used a free weekly newsprint circular to publish a column reflecting on Don Walker. He described Walker plainly as a convicted drug trafficker. He also described him as generous, loyal, fundamentally human, and a personal friend.

The piece did not deny the crimes. It contextualized the man. It asked readers to hold both truths at once, without interrogating the system that allowed such proximity between elected power, the press, organized crime, and public storytelling.

That the column ran at all was the point. It demonstrated how, in Knoxville, moral contradiction is not hidden but normalized—so long as it is voiced by the right people, in the right places, and framed as familiarity rather than accountability.

A former congressman could publicly recount kind words spoken by a convicted drug kingpin and expect understanding rather than backlash. The city recognizes such logic immediately.

The tribute functioned as a civic reconciliation ritual. It affirmed that contradiction was not only survivable but acceptable. A man could be criminal and charitable, violent and protective, condemned and remembered warmly, without forcing the city to resolve the distinction.

Becky understood all of this long before our porch dinner with Don Walker. Her work at the McClung, in politics at the City/County Building, her attention to genealogies, court records, and marginal names, followed the same instinct. She knew that Knoxville did not erase its past. It filed it.

What we were doing—what she had always been doing—was refusing the final edit. Not exposing, not condemning, but restoring sequence. Putting actions back into relation. Letting charity and violence occupy the same frame without allowing one to cancel the other.

That was the work. Not to indict Knoxville, and not to romanticize it, but to show how systems survive by training people where not to look.

The porch dinner did not give me a story. It gave me a structure I was already beginning to recognize.

And once you see that structure, you begin to notice it everywhere—in archives, in obituaries, in tributes, in the polite sentences a city uses to forgive itself without ever saying the word.

⋯

An obituary has long been one of Knoxville's most efficient civic instruments, because it compresses a complicated life into language the city already knows how to accept. Years that braided money, coercion, generosity, and fear are reduced to a narrow, approved register that closes questions rather than inviting them.

"He was active in civic affairs."

The phrase appears endlessly in the record, not because it clarifies anything, but because it performs a function. It signals that the accounting is complete.

Don Walker understood this as well as anyone. Don once told me that once a man reached the obituary stage, the work was finished. Whatever had come before no longer required explanation. Custom took over where law once operated. Death functioned as amnesty. Memory was arranged. Sequences that no longer served the living were omitted. Survivors were named. Affiliations were emphasized. Causes were softened until they no longer asked anything of the reader.

Don died in 2018, a year after Becky passed. His obituary said the most important thing plainly: the family who loved him. It said little else. There was no mention of the statute that had once defined him, no accounting of the city that had shaped and sheltered him, no acknowledgment of the role he played in Knoxville's long, quiet education in how power actually moves.

That silence was not an oversight. It was the point.

Alongside the obituary photograph is another image that circulates quietly among people who remember him differently: Don in boxing gloves, young and squared up, likely from his Golden Gloves days in Knoxville, when discipline still had a ring and rules were enforced by rounds rather than negotiations. The picture matters because it reminds you that before he became a system node, before he became a cautionary tale or a statistic, he was a body learning how to stand his ground.

The obituary does not absolve. It stabilizes. By the time the words reach print, the city has already decided what it will carry forward and what it will allow to settle out of sight. In that sense, the obituary is less about the dead than it is about the living agreement that follows them.

And for Knoxville, that agreement has always been remarkably consistent.

Ten

# THE RIVER SECRETS OF PETER BLOW

We had lunch first, an unhurried midday pause at the Bistro at the Bijou on Gay Street. From there we walked the few blocks over to the East Tennessee History Center.

Located in the old Knoxville Customs House, the building was constructed in 1874 from locally quarried Tennessee marble. After extensive renovations, it now houses the McClung Historical Collection, a branch of the Knox County Public Library.

The building is defined by marble floors, high ceilings, and filtered daylight. Sound is dampened, movement slows, and the space operates under a kind of sacred order. This is where Knoxville stores what it can't always bring itself to remember, catalogued neatly, filed politely, and accessible only to those stubborn enough to keep asking the right questions.

For Becky and me, the McClung had stopped feeling like a repository and started behaving like a collaborator. The longer I worked there, the more I understood that it rewarded fixation rather than efficiency. Becky understood this instinctively. She spread out her materials deliberately, with the ease of someone settled in for the long haul, not chasing conclusions, just letting the documents argue among themselves until something made sense.

By that point, I had been working the case for more than two years—intermittently but persistently—long enough for it to follow me out of the building and back in again.

Becky was deep in her own research orbit, immersed in the Ellen McClung Berry and Dan Tondevaald case, a local tangle of inheritance, disappearance, and unresolved fraud that refused to resolve into something polite.

After writing a book and several stage plays together, we often worked in parallel on different stories. We'd occasionally exchange looks across the table that said, you ain't gonna believe this one, and then return to our respective piles. Becky joined me for an afternoon that stretched without urgency.

• • •

In February 1892, Peter Ethelred Blow left Knoxville on an overnight train bound for Rolla, Missouri, because his name had just been spoken in open court as the man who paid for a murder.

Blow was not the defendant. He had not been charged. He had not been subpoenaed. But in a sensational murder trial unfolding hundreds of miles from Knoxville, witnesses were testifying under oath that Blow, a wealthy industrialist with mining interests stretching across Missouri and East Tennessee, had hired a saloonkeeper to assassinate a rival. The accusation was specific, public, and reputationally lethal.

Blow did not wait for lawyers to manage it. He boarded the train himself.

The story didn't stay contained for long. The Missouri connection pushed outward, then backward, opening a family history Knoxville had never fully examined, one that moved through slavery, abolition, industry, land, and enforced silence. The murder was real, documented, and lurid enough to satisfy curiosity, but it was never the center. The center was what traveled quietly with the Blow name, what accumulated without headlines, and what Knoxville chose, again and again, not to carry forward into its public memory.

• • •

In 2000, the Sequoyah Hills Preservation Society installed a brass plaque near the former landing of Blow's Ferry. The marker honors Peter Blow as an early Knoxville industrialist, noting his operation of the Southern Brass and Iron Company on State Street, now the site of the Tennessee Theatre, and his later move to a 400-acre farm by the river, accessed by way of the ferry that gave Blows Ferry Road its name.

The plaque tells a clean story. It is accurate. It is also incomplete.

After Blow sold his interest in Southern Brass and Iron around 1910, the theatre's owners continued to pay rent to the Blow family. Blow is reported to have also secured a percentage of future ticket sales as part of the deal. He owned other ventures, including a mercantile, and consolidated his holdings at Riverbend Farm on the south side of the Tennessee River, directly across from what would later become Cherokee Country Club.

The land itself carried older weight. The Blows purchased Riverbend from the Jesse Wells family, who acquired it as a land grant following Wells' service in the North Carolina militia during the American Revolution. Wells, his wife Elizabeth, and more than fifty others remain buried in the Wells Cemetery on Manor Drive. The cemetery still sits there, easy to miss from the street, one of the many ways Knoxville keeps its deeper timelines intact but unattended.

Blow built his river mansion around 1910. His wife, Frances "Fannie" Blow, died there in 1913. He never returned to the house. He died in 1945, and is buried in Old Gray Cemetery.

In 1941, George Roby Dempster, industrialist, columnist, and future mayor of Knoxville, published a profile of Blow in his long-running "Like It or Not" column in the *Knoxville Journal*. Dempster, who had patented the Dempster Dumpster only six years earlier, recognized Blow as a man shaped by production, land, and control rather than speculation or display.

Dempster wrote that after Fannie's death, the house stood vacant, and that Blow resisted persistent efforts by real estate men to subdivide the property. According to Dempster, Blow wanted the State of Tennessee to lease the land as an extension farm for Eastern State Hospital, where people suffering mental illness could regain equilibrium through agricultural labor. Dempster framed it as obligation, not charity, meant to align unused land with public need.

The real estate men won in the end. After Blow's death in 1945, Eastern State Hospital expanded instead at Lyons View, just across the river, while Riverbend Farm was subdivided into the Lakemoor Hills community, folded neatly into a great horseshoe bend of the Tennessee River.

Knoxville newspapers praised his decades of civic service, his work on the Knox County Road Commission, his industrial success, and his long residence in the city. What they did not ask was where the family came from, how its wealth had first accumulated, or why Peter Blow once crossed two states overnight to defend his name in a murder trial that Knoxville never mentioned again.

Those answers are not in Knoxville. They are in Missouri. And they are much older than Missouri.

• • •

Blow was born in St. Louis in 1854, sharing his father's name. The elder Peter E. Blow was born in 1815 on a plantation in Southampton County, Virginia, known as *The Olde Place*. The Blow family had held land and enslaved people there since the seventeenth century, building generational wealth long before Knoxville appeared on the map.

The family patriarch, Captain Peter Blow, born in 1777 on the plantation, moved his household west after the War of 1812, first to Alabama and then to St. Louis. He did not travel alone. He brought enslaved people with him. One of them was named Dred Scott. Scott's surname likely came from Mary Scott Blow, Captain Blow's wife.

In Florence, Alabama, Scott worked in the stables of the Peter Blow Inn, established around 1827. By 1830, the family had relocated again, settling in St. Louis. Captain Blow died there in 1832 and was buried in Bellefontaine Cemetery, where many of the city's industrial and political figures would later be interred.

That same year, Dred Scott was sold to Dr. John Emerson. The transaction marked the beginning of a forced migration through Illinois and the Wisconsin Territory, where Scott met and married Harriet Robinson, herself enslaved. When Emerson died, Scott sued for his family's freedom, initiating a legal struggle that would last fourteen years and fracture the nation's legal conscience.

The case that became Dred Scott v. Sandford is often remembered as a Supreme Court decision, a single ruling rendered in March 1857 by Chief Justice Roger B. Taney, declaring that enslaved people were not and could never be citizens of the United States. What is less often remembered is the long chain of personal relationships and quiet interventions that ran alongside the case.

According to *Dred and Harriet Scott* by Gwenyth Swain, Captain Blow's sons, Peter Ethelred Blow and Henry Taylor Blow, had grown up alongside Scott. They followed his case closely. They corresponded with him. They sent small amounts of money over the years to help cover legal fees. Their support was not loud. It was persistent.

After the Supreme Court's decision, Emerson's widow, who had remarried an abolitionist named Calvin Chaffee, returned Scott to the Blow brothers. As Missouri residents, they could do what the Court would not allow. On May 26, 1857, Peter and Henry Blow emancipated Dred Scott and his wife Harriet.

Scott worked afterwards as a porter at P. T. Barnum's hotel in St. Louis. He died nine months later of tuberculosis. He died free.

This history did not disappear. It traveled forward with the Blow name—through industry, mining, land acquisition, and reputation.

By the time the younger Peter Blow arrived in Knoxville decades later, that inheritance had already shaped him, whether Knoxville recognized it or not.

• • •

Peter Blow arrived in Knoxville sometime after 1880, already carrying a dual inheritance: capital shaped by antebellum slavery and a family legacy tempered by abolitionist action. He was born in St. Louis in 1854, three years before the Dred Scott decision, and grew up inside the industrial reorganization of postwar America.

Census records describe him as a lead miner and chemist, the son of Peter E. Blow and Sarah Tunstall Blow. In February 1879, he married Frances "Fannie" C. Williams in Jasper, Missouri, near the mining districts where he worked. For years, Blow divided his time between Missouri and Tennessee, maintaining business interests in both regions.

His father and uncle, Peter and Henry Blow, had formed a lead-mining partnership in 1857 with former St. Louis mayor Ferdinand

Kennett. According to the *Granby News-Herald*, they leased land from the Atlantic and Pacific Railroad Company and erected large smelting furnaces. Between 1858 and 1861, the operation produced between ten and twelve million pounds of ore annually. By 1859, Granby's population reached eight thousand, making it the largest town in southwest Missouri.

The Civil War disrupted the operation but did not end it. In 1865, Peter and Henry Blow reorganized the company with new partners and expanded into seven Missouri counties. The younger Peter Blow followed those developments closely.

When his father died in St. Louis in 1866, Peter inherited not only capital but access, experience, and a map of how wealth moved through minerals, land, and transportation.

By the late 1880s, Blow identified new opportunities in East Tennessee's lead and zinc districts. According to a 1911 engineering thesis by James W. Love at the University of Tennessee, Blow served as superintendent of the New Prospect Mine in Union County, overseeing construction of the mill during the district's most productive years between 1890 and 1892. Love credited Blow directly with erecting the mill that supported the mine's peak output.

What remains unclear is how Blow balanced these expanding interests with his family life. It is uncertain when Fannie and their children joined him permanently in Knoxville, or whether prolonged separations contributed to later tensions.

Census records from St. Louis in 1880 list Blow's widowed mother Sarah, then forty-nine, living with her children, including Peter, newly married. Sarah's own mother, Annie Tunstall, lived with them as well. Sarah would later die of pneumonia in Knoxville in 1897 but be buried in St. Louis, suggesting continued family movement between the two cities.

By 1890, Peter and Fannie were living at 917 North Fifth Avenue in Knoxville, overlooking Caswell Park. At the time, older residents still referred to the area as White's Pasture, land once owned by Moses White, son of General James White, Knoxville's founder.

According to George Dempster, men who grew up nearby remembered swimming there as boys, long before the city absorbed the land into streets and addresses.

It was from this position of security and respect that Peter would suddenly find himself accused, in open court, of orchestrating a murder.

∙ ∙ ∙

The killing that threatened Blow's name occurred on September 13, 1886, in Joplin, Missouri. Dr. Louis G. Howard, a dentist, was shot and killed. The accused was George Hudson, a saloonkeeper with a reputation for violence and consorting with criminals.

Why it took six years to bring Hudson to trial remains unclear. What is clear is that when the case finally reached court in Rolla in February 1892, it expanded far beyond Hudson. From the opening days of testimony, witnesses began framing Hudson as a hired assassin. The real target, they claimed, was not Hudson but Peter E. Blow, owner of the Granby Iron Company and a man with both motive and money.

According to testimony reported daily by *The New York Times*, Blow had allegedly paid Hudson one thousand dollars to kill Dr. Howard because of Howard's attentions to Mrs. Blow. Blow was not named in the original indictment. He was not warned. He was not represented. His name simply appeared, repeatedly, spoken under oath.

Another witness, Gilbert Barbee, compounded the damage. Barbee was a wealthy mine owner and speculator in Joplin, deeply invested in lead and zinc. He owned the House of Lords gambling hall, a racetrack, and the *Joplin Globe*. He also testified that he had once attempted to hire Hudson to kill his own wife. Hudson refused. Barbee claimed that Hudson later told him Blow was the man who ordered Howard's murder.

What the coverage did not emphasize was that Barbee was also Blow's direct competitor. His testimony, if believed, would not only implicate Blow in murder but permanently discredit him across the mining districts of Missouri and Tennessee. Reputation, in this context, was not abstract. It governed contracts, leases, credit, and labor.

The day after Barbee and another witness, Samuel Farrar, delivered testimony placing Blow at the center of the crime, the courtroom was stunned.

Blow arrived without notice, having taken the train from Knoxville to St. Louis and on to Rolla. Neither the prosecution nor the defense knew he was coming. When Blow stood, raised his hand, and swore to tell the truth, the courtroom reportedly stared in amazement.

For more than two hours, he testified. His appearance shifted the trial's gravity. What had been a prosecution of Hudson became, momentarily, a public reckoning of Blow himself.

Under cross-examination, Blow broke down, sobbing openly. "As to my coming here, I came to vindicate my character. I have been charged with hiring that man to kill Dr. Howard. None of the lawyers for either side knew I was coming."

When asked whether he was still living with his wife and children, Blow answered through tears, "I am, and I am not ashamed to say she is still my wife."

The prosecution asked whether he had received any promise of immunity in exchange for testifying. He said he had not.

The testimony changed the case. Despite days of sensational accusations, the prosecution failed to prove its claims. On February 20, 1892, the jury returned a verdict of not guilty. Hudson walked free. With him walked Blow's reputation.

Some of Hudson's enemies alleged jury tampering. No charges followed. *The New York Times* printed the verdict. Missouri talked. Knoxville did not.

• • •

The acquittal cleared Blow legally, but the episode left traces. In Missouri, friends of the Blow family declared the accusations preposterous. In Knoxville, the trial barely registered. There is no evidence it circulated widely, if at all. The city continued to treat Blow as it always had: as an industrialist, a landowner, a civic figure.

Blow returned to his work. He expanded his holdings. He built the mansion overlooking the Tennessee River. He operated Blow's Ferry, connecting land, labor, and transport. He served on the Knox County Road Commission. Knoxville absorbed him fully.

Fannie died in 1913, only three years after the mansion's completion. Shortly thereafter, Blow abandoned the house. No clear explanation survives. The family moved to 2127 Magnolia Avenue in Park City. The river house stood empty.

For decades, the abandoned mansion loomed over the south bluffs of the river. Boys crossed the ferry and explored it. Stories accumulated. The house entered Knoxville's imagination without its history.

Cormac McCarthy, growing up nearby, later described an abandoned mansion on the south bluffs in *Suttree*. The resemblance is not subtle.

The house was demolished in the 1950s. Its replacement, Speedwell Manor, still occupies the site.

• • •

Around 1950, Dr. Frank Rogers and five other investors purchased the original Blow estate. They drew straws to determine who would take the mansion. Around the same time, Rogers learned that *Castle Rock*, an 1830 Georgian mansion in Tazewell, Tennessee, was slated for demolition.

Dr. Rogers dismantled it carefully, salvaging its columns and porch, and rebuilt it on the river site, naming the home Speedwell Manor. Rogers and his wife Virginia opened the home as a public house museum in the 1960s. For years, Knoxvillians visited it, walked its rooms, and absorbed a version of the past that stopped short of asking where the land, money, and silence came from.

In the late 1980s, Dr. Alex Shivers and his wife Pat purchased Speedwell Manor, built on the same site after the original Blow mansion was demolished in the 1950s. Both retired University of Tennessee faculty, they restored and maintained the property with care, preserving the history of two successive houses that occupied the same ground.

I first wrote about Peter Blow and Speedwell Manor in 2009 for the final cover story of *The Knoxville Voice*, a short-lived bi-weekly newspaper. Reporting that piece, I interviewed the Shivers and visited the house, walking its rooms and grounds, tracing how much of the story had already been curated away.

The land remains ringed by trees and water, close enough to downtown to feel improbable, removed enough to avoid scrutiny.

Peter Blow lived long enough to be interviewed in 1941, the same year Pearl Harbor was bombed. He died in 1945, as the war ended, having lived through the Civil War's aftermath, Reconstruction, industrialization, and global conflict.

He was buried at Old Gray Cemetery beside Fannie and their children. His son Richard died one month later. His daughters lived into the mid-twentieth century, their lives narrowing as the city expanded around them.

Knoxville remembers Peter Blow as an industrialist. Missouri remembers a man who stood in court to save his name. The archives remember something more complex: a family shaped by slavery, altered by abolition, protected by capital, and insulated by silence.

• • •

By the time we packed up that afternoon, the McClung was already shifting back into its evening posture. Chairs scraped softly. Boxes were refiled. The room returned itself to order without acknowledging what had been disturbed.

Becky gathered her notes on Ellen McClung Berry and Dan Tondevaald with the same care she had used all day, not because she was finished, but because she wasn't. Neither of us was.

We walked out carrying different stories, but the same understanding. These cases did not persist because they were unsolved. They persisted because they were managed. Names were preserved. Narratives were narrowed. Certain questions were allowed to age into irrelevance while others were quietly archived without ever being answered.

The McClung did not correct that. It recorded it.

Stories like these are never finished. They are contained, released, and contested again, waiting for the next person willing to sit long enough, ask again, and accept what comes back incomplete.

Eleven

# BLUEBLOODS ON THE BUS

In 2005, we had been living inside East Knoxville history for months—immersed in photo boxes, courthouse records, and the kind of oral recollections that begin with "now don't quote me on this." By the time we started Images of America: Park City that year, I already knew exactly what kind of bargain we were making.

I'd done my first book for Arcadia Publishing the year before—the Asheville, North Carolina edition—and to my surprise, it sold well. It's still in print, sitting on shelves in tourist shops, Cracker Barrels, and museum lobbies with the quiet persistence of regional ephemera. Arcadia built its empire on those little paperbacks—one local historian at a time.

The formula was simple: dig up the past, caption each photo in thirty or forty words, and deliver it in 128 pages of ink with a sepia-toned cover. The royalties were miserable—the kind of checks that might cover a tank of gas on a good day—but the return wasn't financial.

When Becky and I signed on to do the Park City book, we weren't chasing sales; we were chasing ghosts.

The area encompassed the expansive streetcar neighborhoods that stretched more than three miles east—out beyond the zoo, Chilhowee Park, and Burlington—territory that had been forgotten, erased incrementally by planning decisions that never looked back.

Arcadia gave us 128 pages to fill; we treated that limit like a dare.

We cheated their narrow guardrails—stretching a heritage format into something closer to civic forensics, packing each caption with more context than they ever intended.

We had one shot to tell the story of Becky's old side of town before someone else got it wrong.

We spent months collecting what the city had misplaced: snapshots of corner groceries, front-porch choirs, boarding houses, barber shops, and bootleggers who swore they'd gone straight. Every interview started as fact-finding and ended like confession.

Each conversation brought back someone the city had decided not to remember: grocers, bootleggers, choir ladies, and the politicians who blurred the lines between all three.

One July afternoon we drove west to Sequoyah Hills to meet Anne Wayland Lambert, sister of Sheriff Herman Wayland Sr. Her husband Walter was the genial TV chef who made regular appearances on WVLT, the local CBS affiliate.

Anne and Walter lived in a 1960s-era condo in the heart of Sequoyah Hills—midcentury red brick on the outside, neoclassical on the inside—manicured hydrangeas, garden and pool views that suggested an order Knoxville rarely applied evenly.

They were old friends. They'd grown up together around Woodbine Avenue, just blocks from Chilhowee Park. Becky had learned county politics at the knee of Anne's brother, Sheriff Herman Wayland: how to haul voters to the polls—with discreet bottles of whiskey at times to provide proper motivation, and how talcum powder on the voting machines verified compliance.

Inside, the air smelled faintly of Shalimar and lemon furniture polish.

A coffee table was buried under old photographs: campaign parades, courthouse barbecues, ribbon cuttings, and one shot of a teenage Anne balanced on the running board of her brother's patrol car, grinning like she owned Knox County.

Becky and Anne reminisced about family and friends, including Herman's daughter Mickey Wayland who won the Miss Tennessee pageant in 1959.

From the kitchen came the rich, wine-heavy scent of Walter's boeuf bourguignon.

Becky clicked on her trusty microcassette recorder as I pulled a portable scanner from my laptop bag and, with Anne's permission, began digitizing family and neighborhood memories.

"Ladies," I said, "I know you both know all this, but I don't. Let's start with politics. What was it like growing up in a sheriff's household during the dry years?"

Anne laughed—a low, polished sound.

"Sweetheart, it was wet as ever. We just called it private stock."

She poured coffee into china cups.

"Herman always said if you couldn't win a man with a smile, win him with a pint," she said. "Lord, Doug, the way people hauled voters on Election Day—cars, church vans, school buses. And after they voted, there were others…" She winked. "Who'd dust the levers with talcum powder. If the fingerprint didn't show up on the right candidate, he might not get his whiskey back behind the church precinct."

"And they might just make 'em walk home," Anne laughed.

I nearly spit out my coffee.

"That's brilliant and criminal."

"Only if they got caught," Becky said.

Walter's voice drifted from a rerun in the next room—"Add a dash of cayenne for color…"—while Anne leaned back and studied a photo of her brother in uniform.

"That was the good part of politics," she said softly. "The bad part was when you start enforcing laws that rich people wrote for poor people."

"Anne," Becky said, "tell Doug about the night Herman raided the country clubs."

Anne looked at both of us, eyes lit.

"Well," she said, "that was the night the bluebloods rode the school bus."

Anne poured another round of coffee and pushed the photographs toward us. Each one carried a little theater—courthouse parades, bunting drooping in the summer heat, Herman Wayland standing on a flatbed truck with his hat cocked just enough to look approachable. Behind him, a banner read HONEST LAW FOR EVERY CITIZEN.

Anne tapped the word every with her fingernail.

"That was Herman's problem," she said. "He actually meant it."

Knox County in the late fifties and early sixties was a dry county that drank wet. Liquor flowed through back doors, barber shops, and "private locker clubs" where the city's professionals stored bottles behind brass nameplates. Sunday sermons denounced sin while Monday luncheons refilled the decanters. The hypocrisy was polite, institutional.

Wayland wasn't a crusader—just a man raised to think fairness meant the same thing for everyone. He'd come up through the sheriff's office the hard way, shaking hands with bootleggers and bankers alike, learning that law enforcement in East Tennessee was less about statutes than relationships.

"Herman liked people," Anne said. "He wasn't some hard-nosed reformer. He just hated the double standard. He'd haul a poor man off for running a still, then get invited to a Christmas party where the same whiskey came out of silver decanters."

Becky flipped through the stack and found a photo of Herman beside a row of yellow buses, campaign placards taped to their sides.

"Did he really use buses to haul voters?" she asked.

Anne grinned. "Of course. County property. Everything's fair on Election Day. He'd load folks up, give 'em a pint and a sandwich, and drive precinct to precinct. If they were still standing by sundown, he called it a victory parade."

We laughed, but Anne's expression tightened.

"Herman built a political machine that ran this county," she said. "But he never learned that the machine runs on hypocrisy. The preachers, the bankers—the same men who toasted him at Rotary—would call him a drunkard in the Journal if it helped their next bond issue."

Becky scribbled in her notebook.

"So he was part of the establishment," she said, "until he wasn't."

"Exactly," Anne said. "He thought he was cleaning up corruption. What he didn't see was that corruption came in cuff links and country-club dues."

[...] Anne leaned forward, her voice dropping a register.

"Herman ran the whole thing out of the Andrew Johnson Hotel," she said. "Same floor where Hank Williams spent his last night on earth."

That stopped Becky.

"You're kidding."

Anne shook her head. "Room 414. Herman said if Hank could check out of there dead drunk, then the county's hypocrisy could die there sober."

• • •

The Andrew Johnson was still Knoxville's idea of class in those days—marble lobby, velvet curtains, elevator girls trained to disappear into professionalism. But by '61, the gilt was wearing thin. The air smelled of cigarettes and worn carpet. It was respectable enough to host power, and tired enough to tolerate secrets.

Wayland's team had turned a hotel suite into a staging room. Maps were spread across the bed. Pushpins marked clubs and taverns. Coffee cups ringed the nightstand. A radio murmured beneath the hum of a box fan.

"Gentlemen," Wayland said evenly, "if it's against the law for one, it's against the law for all."

A deputy shifted his weight.

"You sure you want to hit the country clubs, Sheriff? That's half the Chamber of Commerce."

Wayland lit a cigarette.

"Then we'll get good publicity."

From the window he could see the city blinking below him, the Tennessee River looping dark through the lights. He thought of the bootleggers he'd busted in farmhouses and roadhouses—men without lawyers, without cover. Then he thought of the judges and aldermen who'd sentenced them, now pouring contraband into crystal glasses.

He checked his watch.

10:58 p.m. Go time.

He picked up the phone and called the motor pool.

"I'll need four patrol cars," he said, "and every school bus we've got."

Outside, the buses idled in a row, diesel engines rattling. The drivers—county employees who hadn't been briefed on the symbolism—waited with headlights cutting the darkness. Deputies boarded, checked radios, loosened holsters.

Down Kingston Pike, swing music spilled from the Cherokee Country Club.

Anne smiled as she told it.

"They hit Cherokee first," she said. "Herman always believed if you're going to make a point, start where it echoes."

At 11:15, the call came through.

Unit Four in position. Proceed.

The convoy rolled west—four patrol cars followed by two yellow school buses. The buses looked absurd and unmistakable, moving through streetlights toward a place that had never expected them.

Inside the club, the orchestra was deep into "Moonlight in Vermont." Couples swayed beneath chandeliers. The air carried bourbon and perfume. A steward was setting out silver ice buckets when the first deputy walked through the door and announced the raid.

At first, no one moved.

Then the room shifted—bottles sliding under tables, women clutching purses, someone cutting the record player mid-note.

Deputies stacked bottles on the bar, reading serial numbers. One man in a white dinner jacket demanded, "Do you have any idea who I am?"

"Yes, sir," a deputy said. "That's why we brought the bus."

When Wayland entered, the room quieted. He took it in— the chandeliers, the poker table, the posture of men unused to consequence.

"Evening, folks," he said. "County business."

He picked up a bottle from the bar and poured it onto the floor.

"The law's dry tonight," he said. "Just making sure it applies evenly."

Becky shook her head, smiling as Anne spoke.

"I wish I'd seen their faces."

"Oh, honey," Anne said, "you can imagine. Half the county's power structure lined up like third graders waiting for detention."

Outside, the buses hissed as their doors opened. Deputies escorted judges, bankers, aldermen, and spouses through the magnolia-scented night and onto brown vinyl seats. Tuxedos against molded plastic. Sequins catching streetlight. Someone laughed too loudly. Someone cried.

By the time the convoy turned back toward downtown, the city was awake. Porch lights snapped on. People stepped outside. Knoxville watched itself being transported.

Anne smiled at the memory. "Herman told Mama later it was the quietest ride he'd ever seen."

Sheriff Wayland rode the last bus, hat in hand, watching the courthouse grow larger through the windshield. He knew what he'd done. He also knew he'd never be forgiven for it.

At booking, he ordered no exceptions.

"Names," he told the clerk. "Not titles."

He stood there as the city's best signed the log, one by one.

Then he turned to his deputies.

"All right, boys. Let's get 'em home safe."

Anne exhaled.

"He came home at dawn. Mama had coffee waiting. He told her, 'They'll crucify me by Tuesday. But at least I did it clean.'"

She smiled once.

"And he was right on both counts."

Anne stubbed out her cigarette and reached for another photograph, this one yellowed and slightly warped—her brother on the courthouse steps, hat brim low, jaw set like he already understood the terms of judgment.

"The next morning," she said, "the *Knoxville News-Sentinel* headline ran clear across the front page: SLOT MACHINES SMASHED, LIQUOR SEIZED IN COUNTY-WIDE RAID ON PRIVATE CLUBS. February 15, 1961."

She smiled once.

""Mama clipped it and taped it to the refrigerator. Herman told her to take it down before the phone started ringing."

The phone rang anyway. Judges. Bankers. State senators. Men who had been on those buses and men who knew someone who had. Some called furious. Some congratulated him quietly. A few just wanted to know if the sheriff had confiscated their better bottles.

By noon, the courthouse lawn filled with reporters and political intermediaries working to soften language before it hardened into record. The *Journal* called the raid "an unfortunate misunderstanding." The *News-Sentinel* called it "an overreach." Wayland called it "the law."

He stood on the courthouse steps in the same Stetson from the photograph and told the press, "If the law's too strict for comfort, then change it. But until you do, it's mine to enforce."

Becky wrote the line down before Anne finished saying it.

"He really said that?" she asked.

Anne nodded. "Every word. Herman didn't talk like a politician. He talked like a man who already knew how this ended."

The punishment came the way Knoxville preferred to administer it—quietly, socially, without fingerprints. Invitations stopped. Calls went unanswered. The same businessmen who once sent Christmas turkeys forgot his address. Ministers who had blessed his campaigns preached moderation. Within weeks, the machine stalled.

"Herman thought he could clean up corruption," Anne said. "What he didn't see was that corruption ran the clubs—and the courthouse."

By the next election, money flowed elsewhere. His opponent promised law and order without spectacle. The same newspapers that once called Wayland principled now called him reckless.

He lost in a landslide.

"After that, he went back to the farm," Anne said. "Mascot. Raised cattle and tomatoes. He said cows were easier. They don't resent enforcement."

She laughed, then steadied.

"The irony is, that raid changed everything. Within a few years, Knox County went wet—liquor-by-the-drink, package stores, country-club licenses. They legalized it after they ruined him for proving it was already happening."

She looked at the photograph again.

"That's Tennessee. We punish the man who tells the truth, then quietly adopt his argument."

The light outside the condo was thinning. Becky capped her pen, reluctant. Anne stared toward the river.

"He died in '84," she said. "Still got hate mail every Christmas. But every bar in this town still owes him a toast."

∙ ∙ ∙

The sky outside Anne's condo had gone the color of weak tea. Becky switched off the recorder, and the room settled into that heavy silence that follows a story that doesn't invite commentary.

I helped Anne re-stack her photographs. "Well," she said, "you got more than you came for."

Walter's voice drifted in from the television—"A little red wine never hurt a good sauce."

Anne smiled. "That sounds like Herman."

We thanked her and promised to send the scans once we formatted them. She waved us off, already lighting another cigarette.

From the doorway, I took one last look—Anne framed by lamplight, smoke lifting, her brother's photograph leaning against a stack of cookbooks.

Outside, Sequoyah Hills lay in immaculate order—trimmed lawns, brick drives, river air that smelled faintly of magnolia and chlorine. It was the kind of place that benefited from rules without remembering who enforced them.

Becky was quiet until we reached Kingston Pike.

"This book is our one shot at neighborhood redemption," she continued.

I nodded, watching the streetlights slide past.

"Some ghosts don't need saving," I said. "They just want to be seen every now and then."

"And heard," Becky said.

Sheriff Herman Wayland's 1961 liquor raids were a local act with statewide consequences. By arresting privilege instead of poverty, he forced Tennessee to confront its double standard. Six years later, the state legislature legalized liquor-by-the-drink under local control—not because the state grew more permissive, but because it admitted what Wayland had exposed: modern prohibition was already a lie.

At book signings and civic luncheons, people leaned in with their own versions—who rode the bus, who hid a bottle, who voted dry and drank wet. Legends multiplied, gaining polish with every retelling. That's how Southern truth survives: by being repeated until it sounds respectable. She would remind me every time we'd drive past her childhood home on Woodbine Avenue, and Sheriff Wayland's house just across the street.

She cared so much about the old neighborhood. But it would take more than ten years until the Knoxville Chapter of the American Institute of Architects adopted Park City as its centennial project, citing our book as a primary source. Becky said Sheriff Wayland—and the rest of Park City's long-displaced residents—would have appreciated the irony. Government did something honest for people who couldn't buy their way out of town.

A multi-million-dollar Magnolia Corridor Plan followed. Then façade grants. Then modest hope. Knoxville began addressing the east side—not repairing it, but at least acknowledging it.

Sometimes I think back to that afternoon—Anne's cigarette smoke in the lamplight, Walter's voice drifting from the kitchen, and her brother's quiet presence among coffee cups and campaign buttons.

Herman Wayland didn't reform Knoxville. He interrupted it.

He cracked the varnish long enough for the city to see itself—and decide what it was willing to remember.

## Twelve

# STILL TRYIN' TO SIGN OFF

The letter came on pink stationery that smelled faintly of powder and old perfume. Dolly Parton's handwriting curled confidently, looping, unmistakably hers. She said she remembered the house on Glenwood Avenue, that her Aunt Dorothy Jo Owens might've recorded here once with bluegrass legend Danny Bailey.

"Take good care of that old place," she wrote. "It's got music in the walls."

Danny's royalty checks from Rounder Records still wandered in from time to time—five dollars, fifteen if the postal gods were generous. Enough to prove that a song never dies; it just loses volume.

The house sat on a rise across from Brownlow School, a red-brick bungalow from 1916 with a wide, heavy porch that faced the morning sun. The floorboards creaked underfoot. Someone had added aluminum storm windows years ago and enclosing the upper sleeping porch into a makeshift kitchen.

The Arts and Crafts porch columns were molting sand mortar, their marble capitals streaked with grime.

Old North Knoxville wasn't polished yet—just beginning to shake off decades of neglect and urban decay. Most of the old Victorians still leaned a little. The porches were kingdoms of gossip, dogs, and half-broken chairs.

You could walk down East Glenwood on a summer night and catch TVs playing Wheel of Fortune, the hum of box fans, and somewhere down the block, a guitar running scales through a cheap amp.

The city hadn't yet priced out its working class, its gay urban pioneers, or its ghosts.

Danny Bailey had been one of Cas Walker's men—not just any announcer, but the voice. He worked over at WATE when it still called the Greystone Mansion home, that gray stone fortress rising above Broadway.

Danny had a voice made for AM radio—soft but sure, the sound of East Tennessee filtered through a velvet throat. You can still find him if you dig through the right reels.

"Morning, friends," he'd begin, steady and warm. "This is Danny Bailey, comin' to you live from Cas Walker's Farm and Home Hour—right here in the heart of Knoxville, Tennessee!"

The Bailey Brothers started out in Happy Valley in the early forties—Charlie and Danny, singing close harmonies that could get under your guard. They had the kind of chemistry that only brothers can.

When war came, Charlie shipped out to India, Burma, and China. Danny stayed stateside and carried the act forward with the Happy Valley Boys, singing on WSM in Nashville, then at the Grand Ol' Opry.

After the war, they reunited, got famous, then split the usual way. Charlie went north to Maryland and got into pest control. Danny stayed here, anchored to Knoxville, to Greystone, and eventually to this house.

When Faith and I bought it from the Bailey estate, after a decade of marriage and four previous home renovations, the house still smelled like old lacquer, damp plaster, and pigeon poop.

We found an old WATE cue card folded into a stack of yellowed bills—CAS WALKER SPONSOR READS, 1969. A mandolin pick lay under the radiator, bent from heat.

The air held that dry echo of time you only get in places where people once sang for a living.

Danny's ghost wasn't loud. He lived in the quiet layers—the way the back hallway always carried a whisper, or how the radio would sometimes crackle when the air got thick before a storm.

Faith said it was the wiring. I wasn't so sure.

• • •

Then Miss Glory Jones entered the story.

She lived nearby in a shotgun house with a front porch full of spider plants, wind chimes, and two pink flamingos she'd named Hank and Willie. She was a friend of Danny's—maybe more, depending on who you asked—and she made sure no one ever forgot it.

Tight blue jeans, rhinestone belt, UT T-shirt knotted at the waist, orange ballcap pulled low. She wore her hair short, her lipstick bright, and her attitude like armor.

One afternoon Faith and I were on the porch sipping bourbon when she appeared on the sidewalk, hips swaying, grocery bag in hand. She stopped mid-stride, turned slow, and pointed a long manicured finger toward the house.

"I know that house," she said, voice slow and sweet. "I knew Danny real well."

From then on she became part of the landscape.

Around sundown she'd drift up our steps as if the porch belonged to her, Solo cup in one hand, cigarette in the other, a bottle of Hypnotiq swinging from a velvet bag on her wrist.

She'd drop into a wicker chair without invitation, crossing one leg over the other in a move that said she'd been practicing glamour long before the neighborhood got respectable.

"Can't believe y'all bought Danny's old place," she said that first evening, all statement, no question.

"Yes, ma'am," Faith answered.

"Mmm. Whatcha'll drinkin'?" she asked.

"Bourbon," I said. "Can I…get you one?"

She gave it a slow once-over, eyes glinting.

"Oh yes, honey. On the rocks if you don't mind."

We were both enchanted. She owned any room—or porch—she entered.

"Oooh, child, I gotta pee—don't worry, I know exactly where it is."

Bolting through our open, leaded-glass front door, she shot for the bathroom behind the dining room, which we later learned had been Danny's bedroom in his final years.

I followed her, then drifted to the butler's pantry to fix her a drink, confident there was nothing nearby our new friend could five-finger.

"You treat this house right, you hear?" she said as she washed her hands, the bathroom door wide open the whole time. "Lotta music in these walls. Lotta loud nights, too."

• • •

By December, when our house landed on the Old North Knoxville Christmas Tour, Miss Jones made her grand return—not out on the porch this time, but straight through the front door like she'd been expected.

She wore a red scarf, and carried herself like she'd never needed an invitation.

The house was packed with gray-haired church ladies and young neighborhood couples with babies in strollers, all clutching cider cups. They'd nod at our crown molding and pretend to admire our beat-up piano—older than the house—that we'd found at the Salvation Army for a hundred dollars.

Glory took one look at them, then at the punch bowl, and decided the show was hers.

A nosy, elderly neighbor lit up a black light and pointed it at all of our original paintings.

"Just checking for overpaints," he chuckled.

Another wandered room to room filming our home without permission, narrating the whole time under her breath.

"Get out," I said. "Now. And give me the tape."

Miss Jones, meanwhile, positioned herself dead center in the dining room, hands on hips.

"Danny could sing, honey," she announced, voice booming over the room. "Could charm the britches off a preacher's wife—and sometimes did! That man had range."

The room froze, then rippled with nervous laughter.

Glory took a slow sip of cider, savoring the tension.

She leaned forward, lowering her voice to a conspiratorial hum.

"He was a man of many harmonies," she said, drawing out *many* just long enough for everyone to feel it. Glory let that hang in the air, smiling the way people do when they've loved someone the polite version of the story refuses to name.

Then she smiled, and told a few more scandalous tales about her friend Danny.

The room held—no one moving, no one leaving, no one quite brave enough to break the spell.

After she left, I found her empty cup on the windowsill, lipstick bright against the rim. The room still hummed. Faith rolled her eyes and laughed.

• • •

Later that winter, Miss Jones came back. No tour this time—just drinks on the porch, the air heavy with the smell of wet leaves and fried bologna from somewhere down the block.

She talked about Danny—how he'd sit up nights by the old Philco radio, fine-tuning his voice like a fiddle. How he'd hum through a toothpick to keep his cords warm. How he'd call her over for supper, never saying a word about what everyone else whispered about him.

By then, his body had started betraying him. The chair came before the silence did. Glory said it didn't matter. "A man don't stop wanting just because he stops walking," she told us. She said Danny still wanted to be touched, still wanted to feel chosen. "Ain't everybody brave enough to stay," she said. "I was."

"You know what killed him?" she continued.

"His heart?" I said.

"Loneliness," she replied. "Ain't no cure for that."

Our sound system crackled once—feedback from nowhere. She didn't flinch.

"That's him," she said. "Still tryin' to sign off."

When she left, we sat there with the porch light off, Petty's Wildflowers playing low on the porch speakers, letting the house settle back into itself.

Somewhere beyond the trees, the WATE tower at Greystone blinked its red light through the fog, just like it must've done in Danny's time—a silent metronome keeping tempo with the past.

Dolly's letter was pinned to the bulletin board in the kitchen by then, framed by unpaid bills and grocery lists. Sometimes I'd look at it in the morning while the coffee percolated, that pink paper bright as sunrise.

Old North has changed a lot since then. The porches have new railings. The school across the street became condos. The houses rent to grad students more than broke musicians.

But every now and then, when the air gets thick and static rolls down from the radio towers on Sharp's Ridge, you can still hear something tuning up down Glenwood—a phantom harmony between what was and what refuses to quit.

One night, after everyone was asleep, I went out to the porch with a drink and turned on the old transistor radio I'd found in the attic.

The dial stuck halfway between stations, buried in static, until a faint voice came through. Low. Professional. Warm.

"This is Danny Bailey," it said, steady as breath, "wishing y'all a good night from Greystone Mansion."

And just like that, the house went quiet again.

## Thirteen

# RED SUMMER

We were coming back from Becky's doctor's appointment in Farragut, and I was already steering her big Cadillac Fleetwood toward the interstate when she reached over and put her hand on my arm.

"Don't," she said. Not sharply. Just enough.

Becky hated highways. Interstates, especially. She hadn't trusted them since Mike died.

Mike Brewer, a trainmaster for Norfolk Southern Railroad, had been driving to Alabama when it happened. His heart failed without warning somewhere out on the highway, and the car followed, carrying him forward until there was nothing left to control. There was no curve to blame, no bad weather, no mechanical story anyone could soften or rearrange. Just a medical fact that arrived at highway velocity and a call that came already finished.

After that, Becky avoided roads that moved too fast—places where momentum replaced choice.

"Take Northshore," she said. "Then cut over through Sequoyah Hills. I don't care how long it takes."

So I did.

She'd said the appointment was about her heart. That part was true. But she'd had cancer treatment twice already, and once is enough to turn every blood test into a quiet negotiation with the future. She didn't say that part. She almost never did.

Instead, she wanted to talk about Maurice Mays.

She'd been circling his story for years, worrying at it with the same persistence she gave to Knoxville itself—its houses, its silences, its unfinished business.

"They never dealt with it," she said, watching the road unspool through neighborhoods she knew by muscle memory. "They just sealed it up and paved it over."

She didn't mean memory. She meant infrastructure. Streets laid over decisions. Buildings erected on omissions. Institutions that no longer admitted what they had been designed to manage.

That was how Becky thought.

She was a storyteller long before she ever became a writer. She came from that Appalachian oral tradition where memory lived in the voice and moved when it was ready, where history survived only if someone kept carrying it. I'd been encouraging her to write more of it down. She resisted in her own way. She'd call me late at night when she inevitably lost a file on her computer.

But she wouldn't leave the Maurice Mays story alone. Every few months, every few years, the story found its way back to her.

Not because it was unresolved in the archive, but because the city itself had never settled with it.

That day, coming back from Farragut on roads slow enough to think on, she didn't want to talk about her heart or the tests or what came next.

She wanted to talk about Knoxville.

She wanted to talk about the night it broke open.

She didn't tell me where she wanted to go at first. She just kept giving directions in pieces.

"Not that way."

"Left here."

"No, the next one."

At first I thought she was dodging traffic. Then I realized she was dodging the day ending, stretching the map the way she stretched conversations when she wasn't ready to let anything land.

"Let's go out Asheville Highway," she said. "You hungry? I want some onion rings."

I knew exactly where she wanted to go: east. Deep East. Her old Knoxville. The Knoxville before refinement passed for progress.

"There's someplace I want to stop," she said.

• • •

By the time we reached Pizza Palace, the old drive-in just off Asheville Highway, the light was thinning, the sun slipping behind low commercial roofs and flattening everything it touched. The building sat back from the street without expectation. Neon hummed. Cars idled. Paper sacks moved from window to lap.

Pizza Palace belonged to the Greek Knoxville that had built itself quietly alongside the city's louder myths about who built it and who didn't. Families arrived with little more than recipes and stamina, opening diners, cafés, bakeries—places that stayed open late because newcomers always do.

A low brick building. A gravel lot worn smooth by repetition. Windows that reflected the highway more than the faces behind them.

"I used to come here all the time," Becky said. "This is where people forget Knoxville used to be rougher."

"More mixed," she added. "Greek, Black, Italian, Jewish. More honest about it."

We stayed in the car. She wanted the place at a distance, the way memory works best when it isn't challenged.

She rested a finger on the dash.

"Maurice would've known places like this," she said. "Had a café of his own down in the Old City. You'll help me track it down later. City directories."

I nodded. I already knew I would.

Places like this were rooms where Knoxville's rules loosened just enough to function—where Black and white customers, laborers, immigrants, gamblers, and city men crossed paths without pretending the crossing didn't matter—proximity replacing permission. Not safe spaces. Negotiated ones.

"Rougher," she said again, quieter this time.

"You don't have to tell me today," I said. "About the appointment."

She shook her head without looking at me.

"No. And don't ask again."

I started the car. "Where to, Becky?"

She lit a third cigarette. "They want to remember Knoxville as gentler than it was," she said. "But Maurice doesn't let them."

She paused.

"Neither do I," she said. "Have I ever shown you the old County Work Farm out at the end of Riverside Drive?"

She had. I didn't say that. I liked her stories, over and over.

We drove further east, past the places where Knoxville thins out and loses interest in what it has already decided not to manage. The County Work Farm sat low near the river, built to contain, not endure—brick and timber organized for custody, not habitation.

Becky used to say they stacked prisoners on the bunks there like cordwood. I thought she was exaggerating until I saw the photographs in the McClung archives: narrow bunks packed shoulder to shoulder, space treated as inventory, privacy excluded by design. Men slept fully clothed because undressing served no purpose. Faces blurred not by motion, but by exhaustion.

The Work Farm wasn't hidden. It sat just far enough away that respectable Knoxville never had to see it by accident. Prisoners labored in gangs—building roads, cutting brush, hauling stone—labor meant to disappear once its function was complete. Black men were overrepresented by design. Charges were elastic. Sentences renewable. Profitable. The system paid for itself.

"That's where they put people," Becky said. "When they don't know what else to do with them."

She looked toward the river.

"Maurice scared them because he didn't stay put," she said. "Not in the café. Not in their rules. Not in their story."

At some point, without announcing it, she shifted.

"This is how it started," she said.

And then she told it the way she always meant to write it.

• • •

One of the darkest days in Knoxville's history did not announce itself as such.

Friday, August 29, 1919, arrived heavy and airless. Knoxville was busy rehearsing its optimism. Storefronts along Gay Street hung bunting for the upcoming Victory Labor Day celebration. Chilhowee Park was being readied for speeches, brass bands, and a dance meant for soldiers training at John Sevier Rifle Range north of Fountain City. The war was over. Men were coming home. The city wanted a cleaner chapter, and mistook control for stability.

That phrase had already done its work, long before a suspect ever needed to be found.

That summer would later be called the Red Summer—a season of racial violence stretching from Chicago to Washington, D.C., to Elaine, Arkansas. Riots, lynchings, and state-sanctioned reprisals followed the same pattern everywhere: an incident, a rumor, a mobilized crowd, and the swift reinstallation of racial order under the banner of public safety.

What Knoxville experienced was not an aberration. It was a local instance of a national outrage. It was designed to discipline visibility, punish confidence, and remind Black citizens that participation came with conditions, and that protection could always be withdrawn.

Mays dressed deliberately—tailored suits, clean shoes, a hat worn with intention. He moved through his own establishment with the assurance of someone who understood not just the room, but the city that allowed the room to exist. Knoxville tolerated him because his usefulness aligned, for a time, with its interests.

He moved as though he belonged because, for years, he had been permitted to.

That was the danger he lived inside.

Andy White had once lost a girlfriend to him and had sworn revenge.

By mid-morning, Maurice Mays was in custody.

The case against him was thin.

Mays had an alibi. Witnesses confirmed it. The pistol was never conclusively matched. Timelines conflicted. None of it altered the direction already chosen.

Rumors filled the gaps. Mays was said to be protected by John E. McMillan, Knoxville's mayor at the time. Some whispered he was McMillan's illegitimate son. Becky never insisted on blood. She understood the more consequential truth: the protection had been real, visible, and conditional.

The protection did not collapse. It was revoked.

Becky understood that instinctively. McMillan did not lose control of the city because of Maurice Mays; Mays was sacrificed to reassert it.

By Saturday evening, a crowd gathered outside the Knox County Jail on Gay Street.

They demanded Mays.

When the sheriff refused, the crowd turned violent. Windows shattered. Weapons were seized. Shots rang out. Knoxville fractured block by block along Gay Street. White mobs pushed toward Vine Avenue. Black residents armed themselves. Streetcars stopped. Businesses barricaded. Gunfire rolled through the city until the National Guard arrived, machine guns mounted visibly along Gay Street.

In 1920, Mays stood trial before an all-white jury. Testimony bent. Contradictions were absorbed. The verdict arrived quickly, without suspense.

Guilty.

Appeals followed. Doubt accumulated without power. In 1922, Maurice Mays was executed in the electric chair, and Knoxville recorded the event as closure.

But Becky never accepted that ending.

She finished without ceremony.

We were back in the car, night settled around us, the engine idling. I waited.

"That's as far as I ever got," she said. "I couldn't figure out how to end it."

"You don't have to," I said. "You told it perfectly, Becky."

She nodded. She liked to pretend she didn't like compliments.

When I dropped her off at her stone cottage in Oakwood–Lincoln Park, she paused before getting out.

"Promise me something," she said.

"What."

"Don't clean it up."

I promised I wouldn't.

She closed the door and walked up the path she had chosen for herself, moving slowly and deliberately, while the city behind her continued carrying what it had sealed rather than settled.

The hardest thing for Knoxville to face was not that Maurice Mays had been innocent, but that his usefulness had ended.

Cities like Knoxville have always found ways to tolerate dissent—until it stops being useful. Organizers, advocates, troublemakers are allowed proximity for as long as they can be managed. Once they can't, the tolerance expires.

Clearing his name won't disturb the past, but it can expose the architecture that allows a city to withdraw protection, rewrite memory, and move on as if nothing had been taken.

That is why institutions like the Beck Cultural Exchange Center continue the work—not to reopen history, but to prevent its erasure from being mistaken for resolution.

## Fourteen
# OPERATION AQUARIUS

Becky's house in Oakwood–Lincoln Park was a 1930s Tudor Revival, one of those modest middle-class jewels built between the wars. Its steep gables faced in Crab Orchard stone hauled down from the Cumberland Plateau back when the New Deal was still trying to teach East Tennessee how to believe in itself again. The stone had settled into a warm, mottled brown, streaked with lichen and the gray soot of half a century's coal heat and train exhaust.

The house sat across the street from the Christenberry Clubhouse—a 1930s WPA relic with cracked tennis courts and a flagpole that hadn't seen a flag since the Reagan years. Her front porch had become a confessional as often as my own front porch in Old North Knoxville.

The porch—technically more of an open Tudor terrace—caught the afternoon light and held it like it meant something. Her porch possessed no candles, no marble saints. Just a rocking chair, a chipped ashtray, and a coffee can for roaches tucked beside a twisted wrought-iron railing that leaned toward the magnolias.

From there Becky could watch the neighborhood kids cut across the ball field from Christenberry Elementary toward the clubhouse, their sneakers kicking up dust from a diamond nobody bothered to chalk anymore. The sun flashed off the clubhouse windows and painted the field in hard gold. Every evening around six, a Norfolk Southern freight rolled somewhere out of sight, its whistle dragging through the valley like a long breath. For Becky, it was both reminder and ghost—the sound of her husband Mike still coming home.

She liked to sit there after the heat broke, cigarette in one hand, joint in the other, telling the truth the way most folks tell jokes.

"This right here," she said once, lifting the joint between two fingers, "this is how I talk to God."

She was neither Catholic nor Protestant, not even close. Said she loved both Jesus and God, but the church could go to hell for all she cared.

"Jesus never wore a Rolex or a flag pin," she liked to say. "He didn't need a choir behind him to mean what he said."

Inside, the living room still looked the way it had the day her husband Mike Brewer died—Norfolk Southern calendars on the wall, his cap still hanging on the hook by the door. He'd been forty-six, driving to Huntsville, Alabama in a company car, when his heart gave out on the highway. One blink and gone. A trooper found the car idling on the shoulder outside Athens, Mike slumped behind the wheel, headlights still on.

Her health insurance was canceled three days later.

Two weeks after that, the doctor called. "You sitting down?" he asked. She knew before he said the word. Cancer. Breast. Stage two, maybe three.

"They took my man, my insurance, and my left tit," she said, blowing smoke toward the rafters. "And I had to pay cash for the last one."

Then she laughed—a sharp, splintered sound that didn't ask for sympathy and didn't leave room for any.

• • •

At UT Medical Center the infusion ward looked out over the river, sterile and silent. Chemo smelled like metal and loneliness—an odor that clung to her clothes and hair even after she washed them.

The nurses were kind, calling you "sweetheart" right before they stuck the needle in. Becky said their voices reminded her of Sunday school teachers who had learned to comfort and scold at the same time.

She kept her eyes on the IV bag and imagined it dripping dollar signs—one slow, perfect bead at a time. Every drop cost more than

Mike's last paycheck. The nurse would look at her chart and whisper, "Try to relax, honey," as if the math were the problem.

When she got home, she'd peel off the hospital wristband, hang it on the refrigerator door like a receipt from hell, and go straight for the kitchen. The kitchen was still his—lunch pail on the counter, a railroad-logo mug by the sink.

She'd open the freezer, let the cold rush hit her face, and rest her forehead against the metal edge. For a few seconds it numbed the nausea and the memory of that fluorescent hum.

Then she'd reach for the jar behind the frozen peas—the good stuff, wrapped in foil like a kept promise. She didn't light up to escape. She lit up to remember. To remind herself that her body still belonged to her, that breathing didn't always have to hurt, that life still had a rhythm outside the hospital's countdown.

"People say weed makes you lazy," she said once, as the evening crickets started their sermon from the backyard. "Well, honey, I was plenty productive. I grew my own damn hair back."

That was her joke, and she told it every time someone asked how she was doing. They'd laugh, not knowing whether to hug her or call a pastor for last rites. Becky didn't need either. The laughter was enough—it meant she could still make people uncomfortable in the best possible way.

The first jar had come from a woman at the beauty shop, a friend from back when perms were still political and gossip moved faster than Facebook. The woman still wore Aqua Net and carried cash in her bra.

"You could sell a little," she told Becky, sliding the jar across the counter between a stack of old Country Living magazines. "Ain't no shame in it. Hell, it's the only business in this town that still pays on time."

So Becky did. She started small—quarters to neighbors, hairdressers, and retired railroad men who couldn't sleep. She learned to tuck a sandwich bag inside a mason jar, to keep the smell down. She wrote the weights on masking tape, neat as grocery labels.

"Just enough to keep the lights on and buy my medicine," she'd say.

Not the pharmacy kind—the kind that didn't come with paperwork or sermons.

"You'd be surprised how many church deacons will buy a dime bag if you keep your mouth shut," she told me once. "They call it stress relief. I call it rent."

The cops never came around. Maybe they remembered she'd helped with a city council campaign back in the day, or maybe they just didn't want to see what survival looked like up close. Knoxville had always been good at pretending not to see.

Sometimes, on long chemo days, she'd think about that invisibility—how it kept her safe and kept her small at the same time. "This city," she said, "doesn't mind sin as long as it stays polite."

Then she'd laugh, roll another joint, and let the smoke drift toward the sky.

• • •

Most nights her stories drifted backward, as if the past refused to stay quiet. "The funny part," she said one night, "is this wasn't my first rodeo."

She leaned forward, elbows on her knees, the porch light turning her silver hair gold at the edges.

"I was about 24 when Operation Aquarius came through. Whole damn city lost its mind. Nixon on the TV every night talkin' about 'law and order' like we were plotting revolution from the Longbranch Saloon on Cumberland."

She took a slow drag and exhaled. "We were," she giggled.

Back then, Knoxville was still a small-town capital pretending to be a city. The Strip smelled like spilled beer, fried bologna, and weed. The University kids were restless—half of them marching against Vietnam, the other half trying to get laid before curfew. Nixon's people had promised to clean it all up.

When Nixon flew into McGhee Tyson Airport that May and rode down Alcoa Highway to Neyland Stadium, the bleachers shook with applause. ROTC uniforms, orange jackets, Sunday suits—it was a sea of obedience. Nixon called the students "the great silent majority," promising to protect them from "those who would burn and bomb." He smiled like a televangelist who'd just saved the collection plate from a fire.

A year later, that same rhetoric had trickled down to Knoxville's streets. Federal grants, new undercover units, a sheriff who wanted headlines. The city staged its own crusade—Operation Aquarius—a seven-week sting that turned the Strip into a stage set for the moral majority.

"They called it a drug roundup," she said, "but it wasn't. It was a cleanup—a sweep of every kid who looked like they might vote Democrat or listen to Hendrix. They raided apartments, coffee shops, even the dorms. Half the people they arrested didn't even own a pipe."

She smiled. "And I was nearly one of 'em."

Becky had a half-ounce in her purse and a roach clip shaped like a hummingbird. She'd gone to hear her friend's band at the Longbranch—a low-ceilinged joint just off Cumberland that smelled like longnecks, mop water, and college-age vomit.

"The Longbranch wasn't just a bar," Becky said. "It was a border crossing. One side was the university, the other side was the Fort Sanders neighborhood. Professors, poets, football players—everybody came to the same cracked bar mirror for confession. They said it broke when somebody threw a beer bottle at a Dylan song in '68, and nobody ever fixed it."

The cops hated that place because it didn't care who you were. You could be quoting Marx or Merle Haggard and still get a beer.

Becky had barely made it through her first beer at the Longbranch in 1971 when the door crashed open. The cops poured in like they'd been waiting all week to play cowboy.

"They lined us up against the wall, boys on one side, girls on the other, flashbulbs popping like we were Elvis getting off a plane," she said. "They called it a narcotics bust. It was a helluva Saturday night."

But when the arresting officer reached for her purse, another cop—older, heavier, with a gray mustache—looked twice.

"Hold up," he said. "Becky?"

She nodded, trying not to breathe.

"Didn't you used to work summers for Sheriff Wayland out at the courthouse?"

"I typed up parking tickets and phone logs," she said.

"Uh-huh. Thought I recognized you." He took her by the arm, not rough, just firm. "Come on, Miss Becky. Let's step outside a minute. I need to see you outside."

They led her through the kitchen, past the fryers and beer kegs, and out a back door into the alley. The night smelled like diesel and rain. The officer handed her purse back and told her to go home.

"Don't come back down here tonight," he said. "We're cleaning house."

She didn't argue. She walked fast toward town, toward the trains. Rain started up behind her. No one wrote her name down. She knew how lucky she was, and she refused to take it for granted.

"That was my first lesson in who gets arrested in this town and who gets escorted out to the parking lot," she said.

The next morning, the Knoxville Journal ran the mugshots of sixty-some kids. Becky's picture wasn't among them.

"The charge got dropped because it never got filed," she said, staring into the dark. "One phone call and the paper trail disappeared."

She looked down at her cigarette, the ash long and trembling.

"That night I figured out how Knoxville really works," she said. "Justice here's got two doors—one for friends and family and one for everybody else."

She exhaled, long and slow.

"Back then it was the students and musicians," she said. "By the eighties it was the Black neighborhoods. Same war, different front."

She leaned back, listening to the trains down by the river.

"Nixon said he was fighting crime," she murmured, "but what he really wanted was obedience. And he got it—cheap."

• • •

The names changed, but the raids didn't.

Many years later, when Becky was fighting breast cancer, she had friends all over town, rich and poor. Bearden, Lonsdale, Farragut, Fountain City, Austin Homes, and Mechanicsville—women she'd met through politics, at the clinic or through the railroad union auxiliary. They'd share coffee and good gossip at the Lunch House in Burlington or the Rankin on Central.

Aquarius faded from the headlines, but not from Becky. Every petty new bust on the evening news would piss her off.

Every few weeks she'd pack her jars in a paper grocery sack, tuck it under the passenger seat, and drive across town. She knew the route by heart: Central to Western, Western to College Street, the skyline giving way to low brick duplexes and chain-link fences that leaned with fatigue. She'd stop for gas at the old Gulf station near Beaumont Elementary, and there were always blue lights somewhere down the block, flashing against the aluminum siding of somebody's house like silent accusations.

"It's the same weed," she said, shaking her head. "But when they find it in Lonsdale it's 'possession with intent.' When they find it in Sequoyah Hills, it's 'youthful experimentation.'"

By the mid-1980s the headlines flipped: crack replaced disco; the AIDS epidemic grew; Knoxville pretended it still had innocence left to lose. Rehabilitation turned into Mandatory Minimums. The nightly news switched from college kids to mugshots, and the background music changed from protest songs to sirens. Becky noticed the headlines first, then the empty porches.

"They called it a War on Drugs," she said, "but it was really a war on people who couldn't afford good lawyers. They built whole prisons off the backs of boys who just needed jobs and somebody to look up to."

She saw it happen one name at a time. Her friend Bobbie, who worked nights at the hospital laundry, lost her son that way—picked up in an undercover sting on Western Avenue, half a gram of cocaine in his pocket, three years in state. He'd been delivering pizzas before that, saving for a used car.

"He came out mean," Becky said softly. "They teach you that in there. How to stay mean enough to survive."

The city didn't talk about what happened to the families left behind. The mothers who started working double shifts. The daughters who quit school to raise their brothers' kids. Becky saw them at the clinic, the pharmacy, the food pantry line. Knoxville liked to tell itself it was moral, but it was mostly selective.

Sometimes she'd drive over with groceries and a little weed hidden in a biscuit tin, because Bobbie couldn't sleep anymore. They'd sit on the stoop outside the apartment complex, the concrete warm even after sundown, the smell of frying chicken drifting out of somebody's window.

They talked about Jesus—not the one in the stained glass with clean hands and perfect robes, but the one who sat with drunks and thieves and women who'd already been judged.

"Tell me that man wouldn't've rolled one with us," Becky said, half-smiling.

Bobbie laughed, that short, hoarse laugh that belongs to women who've had to explain too much to too many people. "He'd probably bring the papers."

They'd fall quiet after that, sharing the smoke, listening to the hum of the interstate and the trains pushing through the river valley.

Sometimes Becky thought about how her own name had been quietly erased from the arrest list all those years ago, how friends of old Sheriff Wayland had slipped her out the back door. She never said it out loud, but the guilt sat with her like a second shadow.

"That's the thing about Knoxville," she said once. "It forgives you if it knows your daddy. Otherwise, it eats you alive."

The porch went quiet again. A freight train moaned in the distance, steady and mournful, carrying the same steel Mike used to ride, the same sound that had followed her all her life.

• • •

On the night after her doctor told her she was officially in remission, Becky walked out to the porch with a glass of sweet tea, rolled herself a fresh joint, and sat under the flickering bulb that Mike had meant to replace for years.

She talked to him out loud, the way she always did. Told him about the bills, about the neighbors, about the tomatoes that took root in the backyard.

"You'd laugh at me, Mike. Little Miss PTA turned weed queen. But hell, it worked. I'm still here."

She lit the joint and watched the ember glow in the dark. The crickets went quiet for a moment, as if listening.

"They say God doesn't give you more than you can handle," she said, exhaling slow. "Sometimes He just gives you better tools."

Her laughter rose into the humid night—low, steady, unashamed. Somewhere in the distance, a freight train called through the valley that always made her think of home.

Becky closed her eyes, breathed in the smoke, and smiled.

"That's my amen."

•••

By the summer of 2012 the country was halfway legal and still half-ashamed of it. When I stopped by her house, the porch looked the same—wilting flowers on the terrace, coffee can ashtray, wind chime made of old keys. The old Crab Orchard stone had gone a little darker with age, and the maple out front was tall enough now to reach the power lines. Becky had beaten the cancer, outlived the railroad, and never once apologized for the way she'd done it.

The air smelled faintly sweet; somewhere in the distance somebody was burning yard clippings—or something better. Becky grinned.

"City's finally talking about legalizing this stuff," she said, tapping the joint against the arm of her chair. "Fifty years too late, but better late than never."

By then Colorado and Washington had already flipped the switch, dispensaries opening in storefronts that used to sell vinyl or video rentals. Even here, a few counties east, farmers were putting up new fences and calling it "hemp research." Fields in Strawberry Plains and on the Cumberland Plateau had started to shimmer with that familiar green. The state called it agriculture; Becky loved the irony.

She watched a car drift by with a medical-marijuana bumper sticker and laughed under her breath.

"Guess it's true what they say," she said. "First they arrest you for it. Then they tax you for it. Then they call it medicine."

The porch light buzzed above her head—the same bulb Mike never replaced—and threw a thin halo over her shoulders. She leaned back, eyes on the dark street, smoke curling upward in slow, perfect spirals.

"Ain't that America," she said, half to me, half to the night. "We outlaw the cure first—just so we can sell it back later."

The wind chime rattled—old keys remembering which doors Knoxville ever truly unlocked.

## Fifteen
# THIS IS NOT A TOUPÉE

Becky French Brewer died in 2017. We kept her obituary pretty simple. Rebecca Jane (Becky) French Brewer passed away at her home, July 10, 2017. Preceded in death by her husband, Larry Michael Brewer; parents, Henry and Faye French. She will be remembered for her keen wit, her storytelling, writing skills, and her love of animals.

It mentioned how she always kept a supply of food for the critters in her yard, how she was a history buff with a particular interest in Knoxville, how she co-authored a book with me about Park City, the neighborhood where she was born and raised. The obituary quoted her line, "Home is where the heart is, and my heart will always be in Park City," and quoted me right after: "With Becky, all you had to do was sit back on the porch, sip her gloriously sweet tea, and listen as she wove her colorful account of Knoxville characters and stories."

What it didn't say was what the city lost when she was gone.

The official notice ended the way most do: with her sisters' names, her nieces and nephews, her late husband's sons, the donations to Young-Williams Animal Center and Knox Heritage. A clean full stop. But Becky was never tidy, not in life, not in story, and certainly not in death. She was one of those rare Tennessee voices that stitched together history and heresy without bothering to separate them, and when she died, something essential went quiet.

Her memorial wasn't in a church. It was at my house on Glenwood Avenue—the old place that had seen its share of ghosts already. A crowd gathered in the living room and on the porch that night: historians, actors, preservationists, old friends and necessary ones.

Every chair, couch arm, and floorboard was claimed. Someone brought a chocolate chess pie, someone else a handle of bourbon, and before long, the house smelled like casseroles and cigarette smoke and the low pressure of people holding it together.

That was the night we let Becky speak for herself.

I'd recorded her a few years earlier—hours of her talking about Park City madams and county politics, precinct captains and frozen bodies, voting machines and whiskey, all in that unhurried cadence that made everything she said sound like gospel. So instead of speeches, we played her voice through a Bluetooth speaker on the mantel. We sat there listening to her tell the story of Knoxville the way only Becky could: the version that never made it into print.

A few years went by. The house on Glenwood belongs to another family now, another chapter I'll never read. But it keeps doing what old Knoxville houses do—holding heat, holding smoke, holding stories.

I moved abroad. London first, then Saudi Arabia, then Spain. All of these recordings and notes came with me. The house didn't. When I think back to those years traveling Appalachian roads with my friend Becky, I think of what a kick she would have gotten knowing we let her speak at her own memorial, filling the house with laughter and stories again.

Friends brought folding chairs and Kroger cookies on plastic trays. They left their shoes in a pile and their good behavior in the car. Becky would have hated a formal service, and we all knew it. So instead, I dragged out my little portable Bluetooth speaker, shoved aside a stack of books on the mantel, and announced that we were going to do this the way she did everything: in a living room, off the record, with snacks.

I didn't realize until later how lucky we were to have her voice. A lot of people get eulogized. Not many get to crash their own eulogy.

• • •

Tyler Gregory, a local Shakespearean actor and erstwhile film director, was one of the first to speak that night.

In my memory, he's still standing by the windows in the dining room, thick, tall and a little shell-shocked, holding onto a paper cup with both hands like he needed something to anchor him. Tyler met Becky when she and I were writing one-act stage plays for the Mabry-Hazen House Museum—those summer productions where half the cast was local history nerds and the other half were people who knew the difference between myth and record.

"My roommate Caleb and I were big history nerds," he said. "Once we found Becky, that was it. We'd just find any excuse to sit and listen to her."

He told the room about New York—how he'd gone up there one summer to study at Stella Adler. How he'd see Becky's little green dot on Facebook at three in the morning and send a message, and somehow they'd end up talking for two and a half hours.

"We talked about the Butcher brothers, and then the World's Fair, and then just… everything," he said. "I made friends with Becky smoking after rehearsals, learning about the Mabry family and the Hazens and all that, but… I don't know. It wasn't one story with her. It was just this… ongoing thing."

"I was in New York when I found out she'd passed away," he said. "It was my second-to-last day there. I sat down on a stoop on Third and 106th and cried for about ten minutes, man."

Tyler revealed a small, disbelieving smile people get when they're suddenly aware of how vulnerable they sound.

"History's important," he said. "Not the sugar-coated, glazed-over textbook history. The kind Becky told. Honest history. She didn't deal with bullshit. I feel blessed I got two good years of that."

I knew the printed tributes and the Facebook posts were coming. But that evening, what I wanted more than anything was to put Becky back in the room. Not just what we remembered of her, but her actual voice—the one that could talk herself from respectable narrative into felony territory in under sixty seconds.

So we turned down the lamps a little, and I reached for my phone.

"All right, folks," I said. "Here's Becky."

∙ ∙ ∙

The recording I played that night is the same one I'm listening to now, years later, writing this. She starts mid-thought, as if we joined a conversation that had been going on for years.

"Let's talk about madams that were in Park City," her voice crackles through my speakers.

You can hear a chair creak as she settles in.

"And I guess a lot of 'em are gone," she says. "And even if they're not gone, they're dated. People know who they were. There was Hazel Davidson. There was Bess Davis. And Gertrude Cox. And they ran respectable brothels. Cat houses.

"And that was why you didn't see the kind of crime over there. There wasn't… there wasn't crime going on in Park City—"

She catches herself, corrects.

"There was crime going on. There's crime going on always and everywhere. There always has been. But I think that our people back then were smart enough to think: you confine it and control it."

She has this way of leaning on words like "confine" and "control" that lets you know she's talking about systems, not morality.

"You didn't have the streetwalkers out here, carrying the diseases and that kind of thing," she continues. "They would stay with them. And you didn't see the pimps, because these ladies worked from houses.

"And most of them made them save a certain amount of their money. And on Sunday? They were closed. Unless you had permission."

In my living room that night, people laughed at that—softly, not mocking. It came from recognition, not surprise. I remember thinking that it sounded like the reaction you'd get in church when the preacher accidentally said something sexual.

"That's when I used to love to go," Becky says, warming up. "'Cause that was when they would talk. And they'd cook.

"There'd be a drainboard—well, we called 'em drainboards, they don't call 'em that anymore—countertop, drainboards just loaded with food. There'd be fried chicken and ham and green beans and rolls. Oh, they were good cooks.

"And that's when they let their hair down and talked. If anybody knew what was going on in this town? It was the hookers and the madams."

"They knew where all the bones were buried. They knew who owed who. They knew what kind of crimes were going on, what things were being robbed, or even being planned to be robbed."

In the recording, I make a small noise—one of those encouraging interviewer sounds—and she rides over it like a seasoned soloist.

"They knew a lot," she says. "'Cause they knew who was coming in there in their little three-piece suits out of the banks downtown for a little nooner."

Laughter in my 2017 living room again—bigger this time. You can hear chairs shifting, someone slapping their knee.

"It was a business for these ladies," she says. "I'm trying to think of his name. It just won't come to me. Important, anyway.

"They were both seeing him. He finally fell out with Gertrude over something, 'cause he drank, and he could get into one thing or another, and she'd run him off.

"So he'd go up to Bess's. And then Bess'd get sick of him, or something or other, and she'd send him back. So he went back and forth.

"They got to where they were fighting each other. In fact, Gertrude had one of those Marcel curling irons, and she went after Bess with it.

"She said, 'I didn't hurt her bad. I just tapped her with it.'

"Well, you tap somebody with an iron that's hot, that's pretty rough."

You can hear Becky's grin in the word rough.

"Anyway," she goes on, "they went back and forth so bad that they came to an agreement that they'd just each have him once a month.

"Because they wanted that Social Security check."

The room at Glenwood roared at that the first time. It still makes me laugh listening now.

"And as I said, he was in bad shape anyway," Becky continues. "He finally died. I believe he died at Bess's.

"So they just put him in the freezer. They didn't know where his family was anyway. They didn't know where to send him to."

"They didn't have the money to bury him right then. Or they might've had the money; they chose not to hurry it."

"And finally somebody started wonderin' about that check. Because they hadn't seen him around, and he had to go places and drink. He was like permanently attached to a barstool all the time.

"He lived right next door to the cab company when he was with Bernice, thank God, 'cause the cabs could haul him around.

"So when he started turnin' up missing at the bars, they began, in about six months, to say, 'Where is he?'

"He's in her freezer."

The recording crackles. You can hear her chuckle.

"They took him out," she says. "Lord, that brings back memories.

"But I liked the women, and I liked the stories that they told.

"They always knew when there was going to be a raid," she continues, voice dropping into that conspiratorial register she had when she was about to hand you something good. "'Cause certain police officers would call 'em and say, 'You know, just tone it down tonight. We've got to do our perfunctory raid. We've got to go out, keep City Council and County Commission—' "

She breaks off, searching for the phrasing.

"Keep them happy," she decides. "So we're going to be hittin' these different places.

"Well, word would spread. And when they'd get in there, there wouldn't be a thing to do."

She laughs outright now.

"That's how Odell Cash, when he was in there, had to make a run for it. He ended up hidin' in a garbage can out back. That made the papers, I believe."

"Odell Cash? Or Chubby Smith?" I wondered to myself. I'd heard both versions. Then I realized there'd probably been dozens of men hiding from the cops at one time or another—all over Hazel's house.

As I recall, she shrugged, trailed off, and winked. The room reacted the way it always did with her—amused, alert.

• • •

That's who Becky was to us: a line between eras. She could start with a dead man in a madam's freezer and end up at a County Commission meeting in under ten minutes. She understood that the nightly dance between cops, crooks, and local politicians wasn't an aberration; it was how things actually worked.

Listening then, and now, I felt the same thing: the sense that Knoxville's "official" history—the statues, the plaques, the sanitized newspaper write-ups—was just the clean copy. The margins, the footnotes, the crossed-out sentences? Those were where Becky lived.

And it wasn't just sex work and raids. She could pivot straight into political mechanics like she was changing gears on a familiar road.

Later in that same recording, she slides into it almost casually:

"They think they—everybody knew when they were gonna raid," she says. "Everybody knew what was going on.

"And what was goin' on in what they considered 'roadhouses,' these rough joints and taverns, was exactly what was goin' on in the private clubs."

She doesn't even bother disguising the contempt in her voice when she says "private clubs."

"It was goin' on in the Elks," she says. "It was goin' on in the country clubs. But they were considered private clubs.

"Bootleggers—bootleggers controlled the County government. They really did. There's no way to deny it.

"They could determine the outcome of an election. They could get in with polls, they could get inside those precincts, and control the outcome of elections.

"And so that was bad."

You can hear her pause, swallow.

"Basically, Herman Wayland, when he was elected—he's not popular to this day, in some families—because he was elected sheriff. And a lot of people, as I said, to this day, in those families, hold it against him.

"But he locked up a bunch of people.

"Brought 'em all into Andrew Johnson Hotel so there wouldn't be any kind of leak."

"And they made a raid all in one night. Hit every club in the county—including Cherokee Country Club. Took 'em out of there in minks and diamonds, put 'em on the school buses, took 'em down, and booked 'em."

"He raided his own brother, who ran the Sleepy Hollow—it was called the Senator's Club then—out on Alcoa Highway. Raided him, too."

She laughs again, not unkindly.

"They wrote him up in Newsweek magazine, calling him the 'Eliot Ness of the South.'

"Well, they might've felt that way about him in Newsweek, but he won by the largest margin a Democratic sheriff has ever been elected by in this county.

"And the next time he lost by about that same margin."

There's a beat.

"He did… well," she says. "We tried to run him again back in the seventies, and he should've won that race.

"I hate to go that far, but that race was fixed.

"There were men left off the ballot, areas where a bunch of people weren't even on the ballot in a lot of precincts.

"So he was a character, Herman. He was controversial.

"And I remember somebody said to his wife one time, 'I wish you could get Herman to stop sayin' "manure" all the time. And "bullshit" all the time.' "

Her timing is impeccable.

"And she said, 'You don't know how long it took me to get him to start callin' it manure.' "

We all laughed hard at that. You can hear a chair scrape the floor, someone mention "Christ" under their breath in that admiring way Southerners have when someone nails a punch line without apology.

For Becky, profanity was diagnostic.

She rolls on.

"People say, 'Well, how did they do that? How did they control the vote?'

"Well, think about an old grocery store on the corner. Little kids comin' in, gettin' a drink outta that ice bucket. Gettin' sandwiches, gettin' bologna.

"Maybe they're down on their luck. Daddy's lost his job.

"Or their mom worked at Standard Knitting Mill, and she works two weeks, maybe brings home fifty dollars.

"So these little grocery stores, these little corner drug stores and groceries, you'd see all throughout Park City, Lonsdale, Lincoln Park, all of these neighborhoods—they would carry a tab.

"They'd say, 'That's okay. Pay me when you can. You're not gonna go hungry.'

"That was the way they took care of 'em.

"Well, come election time, when you knocked on that door, and that same lady that owned that store and took care of you and gave you medicine—or that doctor down there at that drugstore—came to you and said, 'I sure would appreciate it if you'd support so-and-so, my good friend that's runnin' for sheriff'?

"I guarantee you, you got that vote.

"And not only that—

"That was a community where the minute somebody moved into the neighborhood, the very first thing you did was go get 'em registered to vote.

"You introduced yourself first; then you got 'em registered to vote.

"And then you followed it up. You said, 'Did you get your card? Do you know where your precinct is? Can I pick you up and take you?'

" 'Let me show you how the machine operates.'

"And of course," she adds, dry as dust, "there were kind of crazy ways they knew how that vote was goin' the way they wanted it.

"They might hand you one of those—what they called an "instruction card."

"You're not allowed to call 'em that anymore. They still got 'em, but you can't call 'em that. Hell, even churches hand 'em out today.

"And that card would have talcum powder around the edge."

"And if the talcum powder was still there when you used your thumb to pull the lever on the voting machine…well," she smiled, leaving it all hanging.

"If they sent that guy in there to vote for so-and-so, and there wasn't quite enough of a thumbprint on that lever when they needed it?

"Well, if he didn't, when he went 'round that station wagon, he heard about it.

"So it didn't take 'em long to get the hang of it."

She pauses, breathes.

"You see what I'm tellin' you?" she says. "We were healed. We had precinct captains. We had the vote.

"We absolutely did."

When that part of the recording ended that night, there was a strange little shiver in the room— the feeling of having something explained that was never meant to be written down.

I shut off the speaker for a moment, just to let people breathe.

"You wonder why she never got bored talking about Knox County politics?" I said. "She wasn't talking about politics. She was talking about power."

Somebody said, "And entertainment."

We passed around more brownies. The night could've ended right there: everything she loved in one room. But everyone knew there was one more story that had to be told.

The one that made Tyler cry on a stoop, that made me and Scott nearly pass out during his numerous retellings, and that made Becky herself cackle like someone who knew exactly who she was talking to. The Sally Hansen story.

• • •

If Becky's oral histories were the spine of the night, the Sally Hansen story was the moment everyone leaned forward.

Scott Bishop took over for this one. In my mind, he will always be standing in my living room with that half-resigned, half-delighted expression of someone who's told this one a hundred times and still can't quite believe it happened.

"This is either 1983 or '84," he said. "Her place in North Knoxville."

He looks down, like he's checking his memory.

"Becky got a new bathing suit. It was Mickey Mouse all over the front, one ear for each girl.

"They were big ears, 'cause they were big girls," he said, glancing around the room with a grin, "but it was a French cut, and it was gonna require a little bikini wax treatment downstairs."

Soft laughter, everyone leaning in.

"Becky went to the drugstore and bought Sally Hansen hair removal wax," he said. "From Walgreens.

"She thought, 'Well, I ain't seen the damn thing in forty-something years, but I'm gonna do somethin' about it.' "

He let us have a second with that.

"She was workin' at Atrium West then, in the shoe department," he said. "Me and Tom were both there.

"We get this phone call from Brewer. And she is absolutely in a sweat.

"She's tellin' us this story, and Tom's on the phone out on the floor, and I'm on the phone in the stockroom, trying not to be heard laughing as she's telling us what's happening."

He mimed holding the receiver away from his ear, like that would protect him.

"She read the directions. It says: apply hot wax.

"Lay the fabric on it.

"Let it cool till it hardens.

"Then grab the fabric and pull in the opposite direction of hair growth."

He shrugged.

"So she waxed up half of it.

"Followed the directions. And she was livin' off Whittle Springs at the time—she had a duplex there. The layout was kitchen, hallway, living room, dining area. It made a circle.

"So here she is, runnin' around in this circle, screamin' in agony, because of the pain."

Then she remembers the desensitizing lotion.

"And she says, 'I'm gonna die. I better use it now.' "

The room was shaking now, people already laughing from anticipation.

"So she pats on the desensitizing lotion," Scott continued, "which acted exactly the opposite of what she needed."

I nearly dropped my drink.

"She's still runnin' around the circle, screamin', and then she has a bright idea.

"She lays down in the bathtub, with her legs up on the wall, faucet between her legs, and she turns on the cold water to try to soothe the burnin' sensation."

And she decides this needs to be reported.

"Similar to that wonderful Kirby vacuum cleaner letter," he said, looking over at me, "'cause we wrote that, too."

There was a brief digression into the Kirby vacuum saga, which Scott shut down before it could grow legs.

"Anyway," he said, "she's layin' there, cold water runnin' on it, she's holdin' the damn thing in her hands—the cloth with the wax and the hair, like something she can't unsee."

At that point, we lost it. People slid down in their chairs. Someone wheezed. I had tears in my eyes and that specific stomach cramp that comes from laughing at something you know is both obscene and perfect.

"So she goes ahead and does it," Scott said, lifting a hand, the way you raise a curtain for the last act.

"And her final comment to us, which absolutely ruined the rest of the day, was:

"Well, now I know why God put hair on the damn thing."

"It looks like a taco with no lettuce."

"And because this is Becky, she can't just throw it away. Oh, no. She takes that strip of wax and hair, sticks it in an envelope, and writes a letter to the company."

*"Dear Sally Hansen,"* she writes. *"This is not a toupee."*

The room roared. Scott had to stop for a second, waiting for the laughter to crest.

"She was gonna mail it," he said. "That's the part people forget. She actually addressed the damn envelope."

"Finally the pain starts to subside a little bit.

"And she's tellin' us this story on the phone as it's just happened, and we are dyin' with laughter. People are lookin' at us across the store like, 'What in the hell is goin' on?'

"She says, 'Oh, I feel better now.'"

"And then she goes, 'Oh, shit. I didn't do the other half.'"

• • •

Even now, writing that line in my small Barcelona studio, I can feel the atmosphere shift inside the old house. Becky would have loved that.

Some stories are just jokes.

That one carried a theology. In nine words, she managed to tackle modesty, anatomy, marketing lies, and the hubris of trying to improve on God's original design with a Walgreens kit.

It was pure Becky.

The woman who could talk about precinct captains and talcum powder on voting cards could also weaponize her own embarrassment and turn it into community. She knew that if she could tell that story on herself, nothing else was off-limits.

The night wouldn't end in hysteria, though. It ended like Becky did: unwilling to sit still or give up the floor.

Her close friend Jennifer Nave spoke next.

By then, the room had settled into that late-hour hush. People were barefoot. Coats had slid from chair backs to laps. Plates dotted every flat surface without apology.

"Becky was on oxygen," Jennifer said. "She was tired. In pain.

"I was in the kitchen makin' sure she got somethin' to eat. She had some yogurt, a sandwich, this, that, and the other.

"I helped her get on her little porta-potty. She said, 'Now don't worry. You're just gonna see a big ol' ass, but I ain't gonna show you nothin' else.' "

Even in the retelling, the room laughed, grateful for the relief.

"I said, 'I don't care, Becky, if you need to go, you need to go.'

"Got that done, got her back on the couch.

"I came back from the kitchen, washed my hands, and she said, "Will you do me one little favor? And do you promise not to tell a soul?"

"I said, 'What do you need?'

"She goes, 'I want one damn cigarette.'"

Jennifer smiled at that, the way you smile at a kid who's asked for something forbidden but honest.

"I said, 'If you want a damn cigarette, Becky, you can have one. But you cannot smoke in your house, 'cause you're on oxygen.'

"And she said, 'I don't smoke in the house. I want you to take me out on my back porch.'

"I said, 'Becky, how we gonna get you back there?' "

If you've ever been in Becky's house, you can picture it: old 1930s layout, narrow doorframes, doors that insist on opening the wrong way.

"Where she was in the back room," Jennifer said, "there was a doorway to the kitchen. Soon as you crossed the threshold, the doorframe narrowed down. Then you turned left and the outside kitchen door was right there.

"It opened in. It didn't open out.

"So I said, 'Becky, how we gonna get your walker through there and shimmy around?'

"She said, 'We're gonna do it. With your help, we're gonna do it.' "

The room was quiet as she walked us through it.

"So I got her up on her walker," Jennifer said. "We literally did this the whole time from the couch to that little opening"—she mimed the inch-by-inch shuffle—"and she stood in the threshold.

"I opened the kitchen door, which swung in on her.

"I said, 'Becky, how am I gonna do this?'

"She said, 'I'm gonna leave the walker right here, and you're gonna hold my arm, and we're just gonna move.' "

So we shimmied around the door. It took a long time.

"Then the big heavy storm door, it opened out.

"We got her out.

"Got her cigarettes out of the kitchen drawer where she'd put 'em away.

"And we sat on the back porch and had her last cigarette together."

Jennifer's voice wobbled there, but she kept going.

"She leaned up against the wrought-iron," she said. "And that smile on her face—she enjoyed that last cigarette.

"She'd quit smokin' about four years before, 'cause of the oxygen.

"But she leaned back on that railing and enjoyed it.

"When we were done, I ran her back in. Shimmied her around the doors. Got her back on her walker.

"I turned around for just a second, and she let go of that walker and flew back on that couch.

"I said, 'Becky, who's gonna help you?'"
"She said, 'I don't know. I just let go.'"
Jennifer shrugged, tears shining.
"She said, 'I'm in so much pain now.'
"I said, 'Becky, just breathe. Breathe.'"
We knew the rest of the story without her having to say it.

What mattered was that detail: Becky insisting on that last cigarette, fighting her way through geometry and gravity to get to the back porch. Taking the moment she wanted.

She could've said yes to a quicker exit. She could've stopped taking calls, stopped telling stories. She didn't. She wanted every last minute, even if it hurt.

• • •

Sometimes, when I think about East Tennessee at night—the way the hills hold their breath and the lights of old neighborhoods shimmer—it's hard to believe that Becky's memorial was so many years ago.

I've moved on, but I've never forgotten. The house on Glenwood belongs to another family now. But every so often, when the mountains go quiet enough for memory to echo, I can still hear that night clear as a church bell—Becky's voice rolling out through the speakers, unfiltered and alive. Park City brothels and madams. Sheriffs and talcum powder. Mickey Mouse bathing suits and doomed bikini wax. Back-porch cigarettes against wrought iron.

Appalachia keeps its own records. The red clay and limestone keep everything. You dig anywhere long enough and you'll hit a layer of laughter, scandal, and ghosts. That's what we were doing that night in the living room—turning grief into record, rumor into truth, and memory into story.

Appalachian storytelling doesn't clean things up. It's about keeping things from being forgotten.

Becky once said she did her best work "in the shadows." I've come to think what she meant was off the agenda, off the minutes, off the record. But records like hers never stay buried. They leak out through porches and barrooms, through madams' kitchens and corner groceries, through smoky back rooms where the city decides what it will and won't remember.

They live in late-night Facebook messages between a history-cracked theatre kid and an aging political operative with a mouth like a longshoreman. They live in shoe departments where two gay store managers double over laughing while their friend screams about her scorched labia on a rotary phone. They live in the cadences of this region—its ironies, its heartbreak, its bone-deep humor.

And if you're lucky, they still live in the sound of a voice like Becky Brewer's: half witness, half confessor, full of contradictions, never boring.

"Goddamn it, Doug," as Becky would say. "Who cares? It's just history. But get it right anyway."

# ABOUT THE AUTHOR

**Douglas Stuart McDaniel** is a writer of Southern civic noir whose work is preoccupied with what communities remember, what they bury, and what eventually surfaces anyway. His fiction moves through the fault lines of American life—coastal towns shaped by storms and silence, mountain communities bound by inheritance and omission, and cities where power learns to disguise itself as respectability.

Born in the shadow of the Appalachian Mountains and raised on fire-and-brimstone sermons, Cold War dread, and dog-eared paperbacks passed hand to hand, McDaniel is a Gen-X writer steeped in regional memory and moral consequence. His work is shaped by the South's long familiarity with contradiction: faith alongside corruption, hospitality beside violence, humor pressed into service as a survival skill.

For a number of years now, McDaniel has lived and written far from home: in the deserts of Saudi Arabia, the United Arab Emirates, and Jordan; in European and North African cities like Barcelona, London, Cairo, and Tangier; and across Brazil, Uruguay, and Argentina. He worked internationally for more than thirty years across infrastructure, urban systems, and global megaprojects. But these southern stories never loosened their grip on him. Distance sharpened them. Writing from outside the region gave him the clarity to return without nostalgia or apology—to examine how power works at ground level, how damage becomes normalized, and how loyalty operates independent of truth.

His Southern noir trilogy—*The Dark Water Gospel*, *Defiance: A Reckoning with the Dream*, and *Bloodwater*—forms a continuous investigation of place and consequence. Appalachia, Reconstruction-era Savannah, and the modern Gulf Coast become linked terrains,

# ABOUT THE AUTHOR

each shaped by inherited systems of belief, money, and omission.

These are not stories of redemption neatly earned, but of reckoning postponed, negotiated, and sometimes refused.

McDaniel's previous work spans fiction, history, and film. His first novel, *Ghost Emperor*, a historical epic set in the chaotic decades following the death of Alexander the Great, traces the violent struggle over a collapsing empire where power, memory, and legitimacy are fought over as fiercely as territory. Alongside his novels, he has written multiple local and regional history books rooted in Western North Carolina, East Tennessee, and Savannah, focused on overlooked narratives, civic memory, and the lived texture of place. His work for screen includes three feature-length films, a range of short films and music videos, and a body of one-act historical plays developed with support from the Tennessee Arts Commission.

With Premium Pulp Fiction, McDaniel writes without pseudonym or protective distance. Premium Pulp Fiction authors are driven by the conviction that places remember, that history is rarely finished with us, and that some stories demand to be told exactly as they are.

He now divides his time between a home on the Mississippi Gulf Coast and his studio in Barcelona, Spain—writing at the edge of the places that made him.

# Douglas Stuart McDaniel's
# SOUTHERN CIVIC NOIR SERIES

Douglas Stuart McDaniel's Southern civic noir series forms a unified investigation across time and geography. Appalachia, the Lowcountry, and the modern Gulf Coast become linked terrains, each shaped by informal power, managed memory, and the long consequences of omission. The setting changes. The machinery does not.

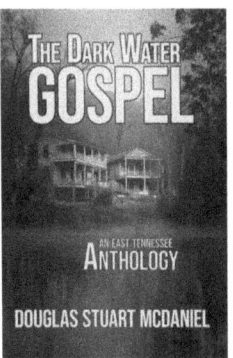

Set in East Tennessee, *The Dark Water Gospel* examines how civic power operates in small communities through omission, loyalty, and managed memory. Drawing on archives, court records, and lived accounts, the stories trace how decisions are made without minutes, how accountability is deferred, and how public language absorbs private misconduct. Like the work of Flannery O'Connor and James Baldwin, the book is less concerned with exposure than with process—how patterns of harm are reframed as isolated incidents, and how communities learn to live with what they refuse to name. The result is a civic record rather than an indictment, attentive to how power survives by appearing ordinary.

Set in Reconstruction-era Savannah, *Defiance: A Reckoning with the Dream* follows Reverend James Simms, a freedman and educator who mounts a campaign to become one of Georgia's first Black state legislators. The novel traces the legal, religious, and civic systems mobilized to block Black political power in the postwar South, focusing on how resistance was structured, justified, and quietly normalized. Similar to the work of Colson Whitehead and Edward P. Jones, the book resists heroic simplification in favor of institutional clarity, foregrounding the lived consequences of law, theology, and procedure. It is a study of how democracy is constrained in practice—and how its failures are later misremembered.

Set along the Mississippi Gulf Coast, *Bloodwater* examines how religion, incarceration, and coastal development intersect in a region shaped by selective accountability. When two sisters inherit a bayou house marked by violence and unresolved history, they are drawn into a confrontation with a charismatic street preacher—and the wider system that shields him. Echoing the civic noir of Attica Locke and the moral gravity of Jesmyn Ward, the novel is not a mystery of individual guilt but a study of how harm is absorbed, redistributed, and rendered acceptable. The Gulf Coast emerges not as backdrop, but as an active participant in the normalization of damage.

www.ingramcontent.com/pod-product-compliance
Lightning Source LLC
LaVergne TN
LVHW061614070526
838199LV00078B/7278